Unwanted *in Life,*

Embraced

in Death

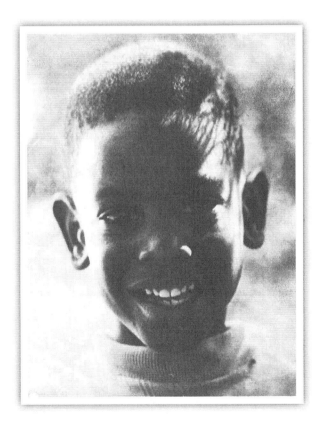

LA LONG
and
NEIL WASHINGTON

ISBN: 1499580622
ISBN 13: 9781499580624
Library of Congress Control Number: 2014909266
CreateSpace Independent Publishing Platform
North Charleston, South Carolina

THE WASHINGTON FAMILY

ACKNOWLEDGMENTS

First and foremost I want to thank God for encouraging me to share my story. Without him I wouldn't have taken this walk and been so blessed while on my journey. I am immensely grateful to so many people who had such a positive impact on my life. I would like to thank the author for putting my thoughts on paper and bringing them to fruition.

Most importantly I would like to thank my beautiful wife, Vickie, for her support, encouragement, and selflessness during our marriage and my career with the United States Army. Without her support this journey would not have been possible.

I am blessed to have two children, Ciara and Christopher. They have both followed their own dreams, and as their father I am proud of them equally.

Lastly to the foster children who are still on your journey: know that you can become whatever you want to be. Being a foster child does not define one's blessings and greatness. And to the wonderful foster and adoptive parents, there aren't enough words to thank you for being a part of your child's life.

Dedicated to all the young men and women who have overcome their struggles, and for those who are still walking this path, keep pressing on!

In loving memory to my brother-in-law, Chevron Pace.

Neil Washington

LA LONG'S DEDICATION:

In loving memory to my mother,

Joyce Lesley Long.

I would like to give a special thanks to Neil Washington for sharing his wonderful, heartfelt story with me and entrusting me with something as special as his journey of growing up in foster care and the trials and tribulations that came with it. May God bless you, Neil, and your lovely family! I would like to give a special thanks to my friend Maria K. Brady for brainstorming and providing the title for this project. We couldn't have asked for a title so fitting. My heartfelt appreciation and gratitude to all my family and friends for your love and support, I couldn't have done this without you!

    LA Long

DISCLAIMER

This is a work of fiction with non-fiction aspects. The coauthor of this book with the assistance of the author managed to journal numerous aspects of the coauthor's childhood memories, teenage years and his military experiences with an exaggerated twist using imaginary characters for entertaining reading. However, names, characters, places and incidents either are the product of the coauthor's or author's imagination are used fictitiously, and any resemblance to any actual persons, living or dead, events, or locales in cases is purely coincidental.

CHAPTER ONE

The last thing I remember was hearing, "Incoming, incoming, First Sergeant," and a loud explosion—and then silence and an overwhelming sense of peace. This was what death felt like. I'd heard it a thousand times before, especially having a vast career in the military and deploying many times. So I'd heard about death a lot. The only difference was this time was *my* time—my time to die! It's true what they say about that out-of-body experience. Coupled with a warm sensation all over my body, this was a peaceful moment in my life. It was one I had never felt before.

So why, God, did this war take me off of this earth? I had so much to live for. As an infant, I was given away like a toy in a yard sale or a possession someone didn't want. I lived a productive life, and now I'm watching my death. I watched my birth and death. It just doesn't seem fair. I've always tried to follow your commandments, even as I got older. I remained steadfast in you, God, and in the word. I taught my soldiers that prayer was a priority. But obviously that wasn't enough. Please forgive me, but I am bitter with you, God. I love you, but I am bitter!

I guess the only way you can believe my journey is if you believe in God. So I ask you, do you believe in God? If you don't, then you will never believe my story. But if you do, please walk with me through life and then death. God has given me the gift of journaling my life from the womb until now. But then again, as I tell my story, I don't know if "gift" is the correct word to use. Sometimes it felt more like a curse.

It all started over forty years ago. I was carried in my mother's womb for nine months. I was born February 11, 1966. I didn't have a full name at the time, and little did I know that I was never going to be given a name by my mother. She had no intentions of keeping me. So the hospital staff started calling me "Baby Boy Washington." Washington was my mother's last name from a previous marriage; it wasn't even my biological father's name. When I saw the light and the faces of the medical staff, the anticipation of meeting my mother and family was overwhelming. I could hear the medical staff; I could hear everything, and as unbelievable as this may sound, I was even aware of the smell of the doctor cutting my umbilical cord. Simply speaking I was aware of everything except the fact that my mother didn't want me. I couldn't wait to be placed in my mother's arms and see her beautiful, excited face anticipating my arrival. After all, I was born healthy, strong, gifted, and cute, if I may say so myself. What better blessing could a mother want than that?

I remember the nurse saying I was well proportioned and, most importantly, beautiful. The same nurse continued to hold me so intently. I couldn't understand why her hugs were so compassionate, but then again, she had also witnessed death often, so birth was still joyous for her. I smiled because she was so impressed with me.

I would soon find out that it wasn't the fact that she was so impressed with me that made her hold me intently; it was because her heart went out to me. I heard her say to another nurse that she wished she could care for me, because for some reason she felt so attached to me and couldn't understand why. Wow! At that moment, I felt so blessed and special that a total stranger was so taken by my mere presence that she wished she could take me home. I smiled because she felt this way. If a nurse felt this attached, what would my parents think? That right there made the anticipation and excitement to finally meet my mother and father even more special.

In the meantime, the hustle and bustle of the delivery room continued. Nurses running around, getting blankets for new infants, doctors making sure vitals were accurate for each newborn, and I was anticipating being placed with my mother. But instead of being placed with my mother, I was now placed in a cozy bassinet—still no introduction to my mother. After an hour, I realized something was terribly wrong. I looked around, and now I could see and hear the doctor and nurses saying that it was a shame my mother didn't want to see me, let alone keep me. That feeling of being placed warmly and lovingly on my mother's stomach right after birth was something I realized I would never feel. I would never feel her arms around me or even see her face. That was the beginning of my life of uncertainty.

I was dumbfounded, confused, and, most importantly, devastated. I was only a few hours old. What was going on? What mother wouldn't want to see her beautiful baby boy? I soon realized my mother had no intention of keeping me; she didn't want me right out of the womb and had made up her mind that she didn't want me after she found out she was pregnant. What was even worse was that she stood by and watched the medical staff hug and kiss me gently because they knew I was going to be placed directly from the hospital into the foster care system. How could she not want me? Did she hate me? How could she? I was her baby! I was the little boy she carried for nine months! Every day for nine months, when she looked in the mirror, did she hate having to carry me? Did she ever love me? I was a part of her. I was her baby boy.

As I grew up, although I constantly tried to understand what kind of mother could let her baby be placed in foster care, I sometimes tried to soften my stance and come up with many excuses for why she couldn't care for me. But what I soon learned was that it wasn't that she couldn't care for me or even that she hated me. It was simply that she didn't love herself.

Remember the nurse who said she wished she could keep me? Well, Nurse Emma was a white woman. She knew that because of her color, keeping me would never fly with her counterparts at the hospital or especially her family and, God forbid, society! Just the thought of that alone made her realize our relationship would never be accepted. Keep in mind that this was the 1960s. Adopting a young black boy in the '60s was unheard of if you were white.

Thank God things have changed in the twenty-first century, where that type of adoption is the norm. In other words, we've come a long way. Thank God for people wanting children who may not fit the typical mold of mirroring them. After growing up in foster care, I challenge people who say how dare a white couple, or other couples of different ethnicities, want to adopt a foster child who doesn't resemble them. Try telling that to a little girl or boy just praying for someone to love them enough to get them out of the foster care system. Some people question gay parents wanting to adopt and love an innocent child, but I would have loved to have been with any supportive, nurturing, and, most importantly, loving family.

Until this day, I still question the ignorance of people who have no idea how children feel growing up in foster care; they have many opinions, yet they don't try to adopt. They have the nerve to question someone else who cares enough to take a child who may never get a home or love. I would have appreciated and adored a family of any color wanting me. You have those who say, "How can you learn about your heritage if you are adopted by another race?" My question in response is, "Where are you when the foster children are waiting with their bags packed?" Just what I thought—nowhere to be found.

At the end of the day, how many foster children like me know the history of their biological parents? I mean, you really can't speak for children like me; you just can't. Somehow knowing that my great-great-grandfather was the only black man who owned two pigs, five chickens, and an outhouse in "Maga-Slap-Me," Mississippi, would not have mattered much to me. Growing up in the system for so many years, do you really think I would have turned down a good, stable home, with parents who wanted me permanently? Let's be real. The historical importance of one's ancestors to a foster child is just insignificant. For the parents who didn't mirror me or have the same sexual preference as me, I would have loved to have had the opportunity to be placed in a family like theirs—just because they wanted me.

Love does conquer many things. Love conquers mirror images or sexual preference. Love to a foster child is unconditional. I would have embraced being placed in a family that wanted me permanently, who anticipated my arrival and was excited to experience my first steps, my growth spurts, my voice changing, my first touchdown, and, hell, even my first girlfriend. I would have given anything to have experienced that.

The devastation you feel knowing someone didn't love you enough to want you or care for you is heart wrenching. I challenge you to ask about my ancestry when I've spent so much time lying helplessly in my bed, praying someone loved me enough to take me home. I used to dream of the day that somebody, anybody, wanted little ole me. Many other foster kids, even the hard-core ones, prayed for the same thing often. All I wanted was someone who loved me and wanted to embrace me as their little boy.

As my day of birth went on, different nurses came in and fed me, changed my diaper, hugged me, and sometimes even kissed me (a gift of love that should have come naturally from my mother). The following day, the doctor who delivered me said, "So, has anyone come to claim him?" I was caught off guard. Claim me? I was a human being, not a pair of shoes or set of car keys. I was a baby, anxious to be a part of someone's life.

But life didn't work out that way for me. I heard another nurse say, "No, we contacted a few social workers, but they are requesting a baby boy with lighter skin tone." Wasn't that funny? No one wanted my brown skin. I wasn't light enough. Soon that would be the norm—that no one wanted a dark-skinned little boy because they preferred lighter-skinned children. I called my skin mocha, but I would hear more times than I care to say that it was too dark.

———

My identity around Escambia General Hospital became Baby Boy Washington. That name was given to me because Washington was my mother's last name from a previous marriage. My last name didn't even come from my biological father. That in itself was so sad to me. I kept thinking maybe my father didn't even know of my existence.

I remember so vividly Nurse Emma coming back and smiling and hugging me. She whispered, "Baby Washington, you will be just fine; God told me so." I smiled but somehow thought otherwise. She had no idea that God had also granted me the vision of seeing my life as an infant and that I could understand everything she said to me. I wished I could tell her, "You have no idea what I will go through in my lifetime, Nurse Emma."

No matter what people say and what race they are, if people have compassion, especially toward a baby, that compassion transcends all, even race. A baby is innocent and untarnished; babies have no racial identity. For the most part, I think all races are softened by babies. I didn't feel the connection to the other nurses that I did toward Nurse Emma, but they all hugged me and seemed to genuinely care about me. Their hearts went out to me because they knew that no one, including my own mother, wanted me. I soon found out that this wasn't uncommon. It just so happened during those last few weeks that I was the only orphan born at Escambia Hospital, so everyone else went home with their parents or family members. There were times when a baby was placed in foster care directly from the hospital, but that was rare. Generally the infant was taken home and then the decision was made to place him or her up for adoption, so having parents who didn't even want to see their own child was rare. So I was special, if only for a few days. I was given more attention than the other babies. After all, those babies had mothers, fathers, grandparents, sisters, brothers, and friends who couldn't wait for their turn to hold the babies. And there I was being loved by the staff.

———

Nevertheless, I was grateful. The staff knew that in a couple of days I would be placed right into the foster care system. In that moment, I was important, and life was precious for me. Couples prayed for a healthy baby every day, yet I was healthy and no one came to get me. I lay there wondering why God had put me on this journey. Why was it necessary to tell this story? What made me so special to bear this burden? Somehow I knew my life would not be easy. But I also knew this—God makes no mistakes. This was my story to tell.

CHAPTER TWO

On the day that I finally left the hospital, Nurse Emma hovered around me like a mother huddling her cub. She kept telling me, "Baby Washington, I will always love you, and I will pray for you, my sweet baby." In fact, everyone was hugging and kissing me. I felt so loved. Just as everyone was saying their good-byes, a lady came in with paper work. She signed a few documents, and that was it. This woman was Ms. Kay, my social worker. She was kind and also loving. She placed me in a car seat and whispered as she buckled me in, "You are going to a wonderful, loving home; I promise you that." As we drove away, I kept thinking why didn't my mother want me? But I knew somehow that I had to accept my new home and what came with it.

When we pulled up to the house, I saw a nice, well-kept home in a neighborhood with houses and fences around it. The neighborhood was clean and tidy. As Ms. Kay got out and came around to my side of the car, I could hear her saying, "Hello, how are you, Ms. Beatrice?"

Ms. Beatrice said, "I'm fine, baby. How are you, and who are you bringing me today?" Ms. Kay grabbed me and closed the car door. I remember other kids running out and looking at me. Then I was placed into the warm arms of Ms. Beatrice. I felt happy. Ms. Beatrice was very loving—she caressed my back and kissed me gently. She said, "Come to me, my big-eyed baby." She continued to kiss me and hug me tight. She said to Ms. Kay, "He is beautiful; he is just beautiful." I smiled because this woman loved me enough to want me without even seeing me first. That was comforting.

Ms. Beatrice asked Ms. Kay if I had a name yet. "Oh yes, ma'am," Ms. Kay said. "Just a last name right now, Baby Boy Washington."

"Well, we're going to fix that right now," said Ms. Beatrice as she bowed her head and took my little hand and Ms. Kay's hand and prayed. "Lord, give me a name fitting my little precious addition." Right then, she said, "Neil, Neil Washington is your name, my sweet baby. Don't you ever forget that name was given to you by your Lord and Savior." I finally had a real name, and I finally felt like a baby someone wanted.

We entered the house, and I remember it smelling like Lysol and apples. My foster mother, Beatrice Thompson, seemed to love me already and was so affectionate—this was everything I had prayed for in the hospital. My time spent in the hospital had made me extremely anxious, wondering where I was going and especially if I was going to be wanted. Now I could breathe a sigh of relief. Someone wanted me, and I was finally home. Thank you, God!

CHAPTER THREE

As the weeks and months moved forward, I felt more at home. I had other, younger foster children around me; they became my brothers and sisters. There were also older brothers and sisters in the household, praying to be placed in permanent homes. There were many days that I felt even more sorrow for my older brothers and sisters than for myself, because the older they became, the harder it was to place them in a permanent home. In the beginning, I thought it wouldn't be long until someone wanted me. After all, I was loveable. Ms. Beatrice told me every day how handsome I was, so with each passing day, I figured it was only a matter of time before I would be part of a family. Little did I know I would wait a lifetime.

Although I loved my foster mother, I really wanted someone to want me—not for the money or for temporary placement or because they wanted to help unwanted children. I just wanted someone to love me unconditionally. I would lie in my crib wondering just how long I would be there.

I also began to question God and why I was chosen to tell this kind of story. It was painful, hurtful, and, most of all, lonely. But who was I to question God? Mama Thompson had several babies in the house, so my time with her was limited. She did her best to give us all quality time, but it was hard; that was when some of the older kids stepped in to help. So if I didn't need to be fed or changed, I was pretty much left alone most of the time. Mama would come in and feel my diaper, feed me, stroke my back, and sing church hymns. She was extremely religious. In so many ways, religion was my saving grace as I got older, especially in the military.

At that moment, I wondered what my mother was thinking. Did she wonder how I was? Did she have second thoughts about leaving me in the hospital? Did she want to die because she didn't bring me home? I wanted her to feel all of those emotions. I wondered if I would ever get those answers.

CHAPTER FOUR

While living in the Thompson household, I always knew there were consequences to bad decisions. The lectures that followed bad decisions were forever ingrained in my brain. I remember one night in particular. I was lying in my crib, and I could hear the neighborhood kids playing outside. My foster brother Wayne wanted to go outside. It was still light out, and I couldn't understand why Mama wouldn't let him go. She explained to him that she wasn't like the other mothers and he would go by her rules. She stressed to Wayne that he wasn't going to be ripping and running like the other kids in the neighborhood and that she meant every word she said.

We always knew her rules were for our own good, but her delivery could crush your inner core. She would also remind us that she didn't have to take us in and that if it wasn't for her graciousness, we would be in another foster home that allowed such foolishness.

Wayne mumbled something under his breath, and he soon realized he should never question Mama Thompson. With a backhand to his mouth, she gave him another reminder that he didn't have to stay here and that she could easily call Ms. Kay and have his bags packed before he could blink an eye.

I could only imagine what Wayne was thinking, because we heard this too often, and I thought when you are a foster kid, what other options do you have? You have no backup. When you are in foster care, you have no grandparents to run to and no relatives that will defend you. You have no one.

But one thing was for sure: Mama was right about being at another foster home where it could be worse. There were plenty of foster kids who stayed with us while in transition because another foster family or, in some cases, their own biological families would beat them, starve them, or worse. So when she said we didn't have to be in her home, although it hurt and it stayed in our heads, we did feel blessed because it could always be worse.

CHAPTER FIVE

Until this day, I will never understand Wayne's ill-fated decision to run away from home, especially knowing the consequences. He didn't run far. He ran around the street and ate dinner with his friend Tommy Jamison and Tommy's family. Tommy was blessed because he actually had a family—a mother and a father who lived in the same household. Tommy was blessed with a normal childhood.

Wayne's unwise decision was something he would never forget. Mama knew Wayne didn't run far. She kept saying, "When that boy gets back here, he will never test me again." Dealing with so many foster kids, Mama just knew the matter wasn't serious and that Wayne didn't really run away.

So she continued to wash clothes with that old washing machine and dryer, the kind where she turned the handle and wrung out the water. I couldn't help but remember that, because her continuous churning on that dryer increased as she became more irritated by the passing minutes. I could see in her eyes that she was concentrating on just what was going to happen to Wayne when he returned.

Finally I heard a knock at the door, and it was Mr. Jamison bringing Wayne home. Mr. Jamison said, "Ms. Beatrice, this is a fine young man you have here, and his manners are out of this world. Me and Joyce just love having him around. You have done a great job with him! Yes, ma'am, you are a blessing to these kids' lives."

Mama thanked him and said, "Well, thank you, Jimmy. I appreciate you and Joyce seeing that I do my best with these kids, especially the troubled ones."

At that moment, I knew Wayne was in for an unpleasant evening. He wasn't troubled. He just wanted some love and affection from a family who cared. Mama continued to thank Mr. Jamison as she grabbed Wayne around the shoulder and told him to go take a bath. I realized then that Mr. Jamison had no idea that Wayne ran away. Of course he hadn't known, or he would have brought him home sooner. Once again Mama thanked him for bringing her baby home. She then said, "Tell Mable I send my prayers. I heard she's recovering from hip surgery." (Mable was Mr. Jamison's mother).

Mr. Jamison replied, "I'll surely tell her, Ms. Beatrice."

Mama was grinning and smiling, and I knew her niceties in front of Mr. Jamison were just temporary. "Good night, Jimmy. Tell Joyce I said thank you." Then she closed the door. My heart fell to the ground because I knew Wayne was in big trouble. I could hear Wayne running his bath water. I could even hear him crying. He knew he was about to get Mama's wrath. I wondered again how he could have done something so crazy, because he knew it wasn't going to end in his favor. But desperation could make even someone like Wayne tangle with consequences, including Mama's.

I kept wondering if Mama ever thought that Wayne just wanted to experience a normal dinner with a two-parent household and parents asking how his day at school was. Not that Mama didn't care about our school days, but sometimes we just wanted some normalcy; for instance, some one-on-one involvement or a choice as to what we wanted on our plates for dinner. But instead, all we ever got from Mama Thompson was the same old comment of, "This is what I cooked, and if you don't want it, then go to bed hungry." We never had any say-so whatsoever. We didn't even have a father figure to talk to about something as a simple as getting a haircut.

Mr. Jamison really liked Wayne; he was like a surrogate father to him. When he took Tommy for a haircut, he would always come and ask Mama if he could take Wayne. I'm sure this was the only time Wayne felt some normalcy and that there was a family out there who cared for him, a family who wanted to spend time and include him as if he was their own, even if they were a "borrowed" family. But Mama didn't think that way. She felt Wayne knew the rules yet purposely disobeyed her. She felt it was a slap in her face for us to favor others, and she always reminded us to never disobey her, because she was doing us a favor. Most importantly, we should be grateful at all times! The sad part was we *were* grateful, but nevertheless, we heard that more times than we cared to think about.

———

As Wayne continued to cry, I cried for him. Mama told him to get his ass in the tub. The more he cried, the madder it made her. As soon as he got in the tub, she told him to get out. That meant one thing—she wanted Wayne to feel whatever was coming to him in a way that was as devastating as possible. He hesitated. I could hear her pulling him out and the sound of the water swishing violently. Then all hell broke loose. She beat him with an extension cord. He screamed. The more he screamed, the more she beat him and yelled for him to shut up.

The more she beat him, the more I cried for him. I couldn't take it anymore; I just cried myself to sleep. Wayne was beaten until he fell to the floor. He shed no more tears and didn't even try to avoid Mama's wrath with the cord. He became lifeless; he had given up. This may have been in his best interest. Mama Thompson was no young woman; she had to be tired. After all, she had chased and beaten this boy for five minutes. Five minutes may not seem long, but try telling that to the little boy who was beaten until he bled. My heart ached for my brother. But what could I do?

CHAPTER SIX

The next morning everything seemed to settle. I vividly remember Wayne coming in the room that I shared with my foster brother and sister. He rubbed my hand. His eyes were still puffy. I was overwhelmed with sadness. Wayne sat down next to the crib. I could tell he was in excruciating pain; nevertheless, he still mustered up a smile. I kept thinking how could he not see I understood this? Couldn't he see in my face that I had this gift? I often wondered when he looked at me if he ever noticed that my expression was not one of a baby. But then again, his expression was not that of a nine-year-old either.

I felt myself shaking and crying all over again. Wayne didn't pick me up because Mama wouldn't approve, so he stood next to the crib and bent down and hugged me. I wanted to tell him that I loved him. He was so sad that I could feel his sadness. I prayed Mama didn't come in the room, because this too would have been grounds for punishment.

Somehow I think Wayne knew I was different. I remember him whispering, "Neil, I hope and pray you don't stay here as long as I've been here." Wayne was only nine but had the world on his little shoulders; he talked so maturely for his age. He definitely had an old soul, even older than some of the older kids. Maybe I noticed Wayne more because he was too old to hang with the younger kids and too little to hang with the older ones.

My brother was compassionate. The one consolation from being in foster care was that he always seemed filled with joy when I smiled so big whenever he came into the room. It made him feel loved. Little did he know that I could feel his pain and heartache. I knew in his heart that he never felt loved or wanted, but I wanted him. I couldn't express this because I was just a baby, but I prayed that in his heart he felt my love. I always tried to express it the best way I could so that he would notice. I prayed he could see my eyes light up when he came into the room or when he tickled me and made me giggle. There were times when not even Mama could console me when I was crying. But all Wayne had to do was come in and stroke my arm, and I would stop crying immediately. I prayed he could somehow feel my love, if only for a moment. I couldn't explain my connection to Wayne, but it was so heartfelt.

Eventually I found out the connection between me and Wayne was so much deeper than on the surface. Wayne was the brother of a newborn who was also placed in foster care, just not in the Thompson home. Only God knew where Wayne's baby brother ended up. The one thing that stuck out in my mind was at least Wayne's mother tried to keep them. But once she got pregnant again, she just gave up. I don't know what is worse—being given up at birth or knowing and loving someone for six years and then having them give you away. I imagine both are devastating. So in Wayne's heart, I was the brother who was given away.

That night, I prayed for me and Wayne. I prayed that we would get a mother and father, be placed together, and he would always be my big brother.

CHAPTER SEVEN

The years passed, and my new excitement as a five-year-old was antici-pating the Head Start program. I watched as Wayne, my other foster brother, Eric, and the others went to school. Besides another baby who was sent to Mama in the last few months, Carole and I were the young-est. I finally felt like a big boy. Now that everyone was at school, I was the eldest in the household. And you better believe I let the younger ones know! I was becoming more vocal and confident.

Carole was a handful; she was downright mean. There were times when she would spit on me, hit me, and try to boss me around. Mama always taught us boys to never lay a hand on a girl. She told us if we started hitting girls when we were small, it would follow us in our adult lives. I took that advice to heart. Even though Carole took me to the edge many times, I never hit her. And that lesson not to ever lay a hand on a female would last me a lifetime.

There were other things that would last a lifetime, even funny things sometimes. Once I had two loose teeth, so I decided, being the genius that I am, to tie a string to the bottom of both teeth and attach the string to a tree. I asked the kids to pull me away from the tree. And booyah! Just like that I felt the pain, and not one but both teeth came flying out of my mouth. I was in a daze. I was not only in pain, but I was terrified of what Mama would do. So without hesitation, all of the kids and I started looking for my teeth in the yard frantically.

Needless to say, we never found those suckers. Don't ask me what I thought I was going to do if I found them; I couldn't glue them back in. Mama found out and, to my surprise, comforted me. She held me in her arms and explained that I should have never done that, but the tooth fairy would still come. Mama definitely had her moments, but that day she was pure love.

A few weeks later when the social worker came by, I heard Mama telling her what had happened; they thought it was hysterical. Mama assured the social worker that she felt that the older kids had put me up to it, so she didn't punish me. When you thought you would be in trouble, she could surprise you.

I also remember one Sunday Mama didn't feel good, but she still made us go to church; that was a must. Some older foster sisters took us younger kids. I guess you could say I was a little bit more jittery and felt a sense of cool since Mama wasn't around, so I started talking, knowing full well that I shouldn't, and before I knew it, my foster sister had hit me in the mouth with her pocketbook.

I was so aggravated I couldn't wait to tell Mama, although it could have backfired since I was talking in church. But to my surprise, Mama was upset with my sister and popped her in the mouth with the same purse. I was elated, yet a little taken aback that Mama had my back.

But my luck would soon run out. Mama had told me not to go play with my friend in the old cars parked across the street. Mama always complained, "Those damn neighbors need to get them damn cars out the yards and send them to the junkyard where they belong." But hell, after two close calls and still no punishment, I pushed my luck again. When I got back, Mama asked me, "Neil, where have you been?" I lied and said that I was playing around in the yard across the street. But with a slap across my face that I thought would sting the rest of my life, Mama Thompson told me she smelled the old cars on my clothes and body. So that day I realized I had pushed my luck one too many times.

As I got older, Mama started teaching us about taking care of our clothes. I appreciated and understood why she would make the big kids change their clothes immediately when they got home from school. We were taught the value of nice clothes and to make sure we took care of them, even if they were hand-me-downs at times.

One day, a different social worker came over to take pictures and talk to Mama about how I was behaving and what type of child I was. I kept wondering why she continued to ask these questions when all she had to do was read Ms. Kay's profile of me. That was why I loved Ms. Kay. She was kind. She made me feel safe. I always felt wanted with her, and when she asked questions, they weren't so impersonal; they were kind and caring.

Nevertheless, I was told to get dressed up. Mama made me wear one of my best outfits. I found myself posing and even enjoying this brief moment of attention. I laughed a lot and smiled. I kept thinking, Neil, take the best, most loving pictures you can and show the funny side of you. I thought if I looked really good and seemed funny, a family would want me. I felt confident that I looked my very best.

But that moment of excitement and confidence didn't last long. Mama told me, "Neil, go and take your clothes off, and I will be in to help you in a minute."

I remember hearing the evaluation of the social worker as she talked to Mama. "The pictures turned out quite well, Ms. Thompson," she said. "Neil is all mouth and ears. He also has very kinky hair and dark skin. Ms. Thompson, what we're finding out is that ninety-five percent of the time, we are requested to find light-skinned children with, how do I say this without offending you—umm, nicer hair."

Mama replied, "I understand; I've been in this business a long time, so I know whatcha mean." What hurt me even more was when I heard Mama say, "I understand because my biological son is 'high yella' and has green eyes. There's not a black or white person around who doesn't think he's adorable." She continued to laugh and said, "And my Neil is always using that big ole mouth of his; sometimes I wish that boy would shut up. God knows I do." Then she laughed.

I was devastated. My heart was consumed with betrayal. I enjoyed taking the pictures. I was polite, and I was happy. I felt my wonderful qualities would show through. After seeing my pictures, I had thought there was no way a family wouldn't want me. But after listening to two people mock my appearance, I wasn't so sure anymore. What hurt the most was the fact that Mama giggled with this woman and agreed wholeheartedly about me always running my big mouth. I thought Mama enjoyed when I talked to her and sang the church songs that she taught me. My ears might not have fit my head at the time, but I would grow into them, and I thought I was handsome. No one was going to make me feel any less.

I took off my socks and sat on the bed. I couldn't move. I was so hurt. How could grown-ups say such hurtful things? Did they ever think that their words could stick to a child's heart forever? Finally Mama came in the bedroom and said, "Take them clothes off, boy. I don't want you to get them dirty." I wanted to tell her that I understood her and she hurt me. But of course I couldn't.

CHAPTER EIGHT

Although Mama believed in God, I often wondered if it was more on the surface than true conviction. If she believed in God, how could she beat Wayne so severely that he almost passed out? How could she mock my looks if she truly loved me? How could she not understand that we were children who got tired of hearing that if it wasn't for her, God knows where we would be? Although I did appreciate being placed at her house after my birth, I still questioned her motives.

That day of the pictures, I continued to take my clothes off with her help. With all the hurt in my heart and questions regarding her actions, I crawled in bed. She came back a few minutes later and felt my head and asked me, "Neil, baby, you're not getting sick on me, are you?" I looked at her and thought she had no idea how sick I really was.

That evening Mama made me get up so I could get washed up for dinner. The funny thing was all the kids knew something was wrong. I was lethargic and lifeless. I couldn't shake my feelings from that afternoon. I kept thinking was everyone going to think I had big ears, a big mouth, coarse hair, and dark skin? Is this what I had to look forward to the rest of my life—people mocking my appearance? Were people going to judge me without getting to know how special I really was? Were they just going to pass me by without realizing I was smart, funny, happy, lovable, and, most of all, handsome? If nobody was going to tell me how handsome I was, I would have to keep telling myself. If only someone would give me a chance, I would be the best little boy I could be. I would be polite and adore my parents. I kept praying that eventually someone would see it in my eyes or in my pictures and give me a chance. They just had to see it.

Later, Wayne came in to check on me. He pulled my leg and said, "Neil, you are a peel; that's my new name for you." And I couldn't help but smile. He pulled a chair next to the window and said, "Neil the Peel, come over here, little brother. Let's count how many stars there are in the sky."

I counted as many as I could without giving away that I knew a lot more than I should. I hated not being able to tell Wayne my secret, but God had his reasons. I was sure Wayne wouldn't have been able to understand this himself. Even grown-ups wouldn't have been able to understand this. We continued to count stars, and I looked at Wayne and felt overwhelmed. At least I had him, but he didn't have anyone to make his bad days better. He was my protector. As Wayne looked toward the sky, he explained that he learned about the stars in school and wanted us to find the Big Dipper.

The moon was huge that night. It lit up the sky. It was a peaceful night, and I welcomed it. I didn't even think much about what had happened earlier in the day, because Wayne's love and compassion had such an effect on me. He could make all wrongs right with the world for me. I could see him praying.

He grabbed my hand and said, "Peel, bow your head, little brother, and let's pray." I looked at him and did what I was told. He began to pray, "God, I beg of you to let me and Neil find a good home with parents that want the both of us. I don't want to leave Neil here. But if I don't get another home soon, God, I don't know if I can continue on. So please... please hear me. I'm a good boy, and Neil's a good baby. Just let my mom come back with my little brother, and let her want the three of us. Please, God, please. Amen. Say amen, Neil."

"Amen," I said.

"C'mon, Neil the Peel, let me tuck you in bed before Mama knows we're still up," he said. I smiled and hugged him and kissed him on the cheek. He looked surprised, but I could tell it made him happy.

My heart was heavy. I couldn't take any more of this little guy's sadness. I didn't want this gift. I didn't want to continue to hurt. At that moment, I prayed to God, "Please let me go through this journey without more pain and, most importantly, with understanding." I continued praying. "God, I know this is my journey and you feel I should follow it. Obviously you thought I was strong enough, but it hurts too much. I beg of you, Lord, please release me from this insight."

But God spoke to me that night and said, "I chose you because I know what's best. I will never leave you nor forsake you. You will continue this journey until I say otherwise, my son. Just like my son endured the worst of pain and I could have stopped that; what makes you think I should lessen your pain and, most importantly, your journey? You will see. I will not leave you, my son." Although I continued to cry that night, my heart was no longer heavy. I had to accept this burden at hand, because who was I to question God? I was no one, this little boy on this journey.

CHAPTER NINE

The days passed slowly, and my excitement about going to school was even greater because I would finally be following Eric. Although my greatest connection was to Wayne, I loved Eric, and being so close in age, we had so much in common. We pretty much shared everything. When Eric went to school I cried, because somehow, it didn't seem fair. I remember Mama telling Ms. Kay that I was so stubborn that I would stay mad all day, staring out of the window, waiting for the kids to come home one by one. I was always excited when I finally saw Eric. He would tell me what had happened in school, and then we would play together. But my real excitement was when I saw Wayne.

Every day after school, Wayne would make a beeline to pick me up and hug me. He always made a point to say, "Neil, were you good for Mama?" I would hug him and nod my head yes. Although he knew he would be in trouble with Mama, he would sneak me a piece of candy from time to time. He would tell me, "Don't tell, and chew fast." And of course I would.

Wayne was now fourteen years old, and I was five. I would watch him do his homework. Often he would give me a pencil and paper and let me practice writing my name. He was so patient. He would hold my hand and show me how to print my name.

In a few more months, it would be my turn to start school. I couldn't wait. Mama also started sitting down with me more to show me how to print my name. This was one of the times when I felt more loved because the attention now shifted to me.

Ms. Kay was coming around more often to bring supply vouchers for school. Certain days were more special in the Thompson household. Mama always kept a tidy home, but on the days the social worker was going to visit, things were picture-perfect. For the most part, Eric, Carole, and I still had Ms. Kay as our social worker. I adored Ms. Kay because she was so patient and loving. Her facial expressions and emotions when Mama would say negative things about us made me wonder if she was beginning to see Mama for who she really was.

It seemed Ms. Kay was beginning to question some of Mama's answers when she talked about us. Once Mama mentioned that I was so stubborn, and Ms. Kay said, "Well, Ms. Beatrice, he is growing up and coming into his own."

But that didn't deter Mama from getting her point across or the last word. Quickly replying, Mama said, "He can be stubborn if he wants; you will be getting a call to fetch this boy." Then she let out her irritating laugh.

I questioned Mama's intentions and if in fact she would call Ms. Kay for Eric if she thought he was mouthing off. I wondered this because Eric seemed to be becoming Mama's favorite. I tried to ignore it, but it seemed to be true. It hurt. But that day Ms. Kay just smiled at Mama and said, "Neil is a good boy. If I come for him, it will be because some lucky family wants him." I smiled because that made me feel wanted.

On days when Ms. Kay came to the house, we were encouraged to tell her how happy Mama Thompson made us. We were also encouraged to let Ms. Kay know we got new clothes, toys, or anything good from our caretaker. We would get pampered, if only for that day. Mama really couldn't understand that we were smarter than she gave us credit for.

There were days when we got a beating for asking a question, but then all of a sudden we were supposed to forget the bad things that happened to us because the social worker was coming.

But for now, I would take one day of pampering, being allowed to eat special cookies and receiving an unexpected hug that I never received otherwise. I always loved to see Ms. Kay; besides, she'd been with me longer than my foster mother. Ms. Kay was caring; she wasn't like some of the other social workers who were in it to get a paycheck. She was sincere. I couldn't pinpoint why this woman meant so much to me, but I was sure in time I would.

I know all social workers aren't in it for the money, but sometimes their insensitive words made me think that. I felt Ms. Kay truly loved me. Sometimes she would bring us little forget-me-nots. Call it wishful thinking, but to me, mine was always special. Remembering my birthday, she brought me a red sweater. Mama had gotten me a red wagon—well, it wasn't mine exactly because I always had to share my gifts with my foster brothers and sister, but nevertheless, it was mine for a day. My red wagon and sweater launched my fascination with the color red, which would last a lifetime.

I would sit on Ms. Kay's lap, and she would stroke my back the way I wanted Mama to do. Mama wasn't very affectionate, but she was a good mother in hindsight. On the day she gave me the sweater, Ms. Kay asked me, "Neil, did you have a special birthday?" And overall I did.

I didn't mention that I was sent to bed early because Mama thought I wasn't grateful enough. As I lay in bed that night, I thought how grateful could a five-year-old be? I was excited and happy; I thought I had enjoyed my day to the fullest. But certain things would set Mama off, and you never knew what they would be. On one visit, Ms. Kay mentioned to Mama that she would be picking Eric, Carole, and me up the following week for a showing. A showing was when we got dressed in our finest clothes, not our school clothes but our let-us-show-you-how-good-we-look-and-pray-we-look-so-good-you-want-to-take-us-home clothes.

During a showing, we were taken down to the social worker's office for a more in-depth observation, sometimes a small tea party and, at times, conversations. More pictures for potential permanent-placement candidates were taken. I always felt anxious and scared during these trips. It wasn't like getting the pictures taken at home; it was more pressure and more intense. Sometimes I felt it was a trick and I wasn't going back home. But there were times when I actually met potential parents, and the showings were more invasive. People would turn me around, open my mouth, touch my hair, and pick me up. They did whatever they wanted to do to see if I was the kid for them.

CHAPTER TEN

Obviously I never passed. The word "showing" always bothered me, because it sounded like something a Realtor did for a house. I kept thinking we were simply property that couldn't be sold or unloaded. But we weren't property; we were loving human beings. Eventually I got used to the word "showing" and the disappointments. There were times I wanted to tell them, "I hear you; I'm listening to every hurtful comment you're making about my appearance." As a young child, I assumed adults would have more discretion, but they didn't. As a foster child, I became a voice unheard. That feeling of being looked at as merchandise sometimes consumed me. Although God gave me this so-called gift, imagine feeling this pain and understanding it.

What kind of God would want me to endure this pain? On one visit I remember one of the social workers commenting, "These kids come from the Thompson household, right?"

Ms. Kay replied, "Yes, all three."

And with a quick swipe of her pen, the social worker said, "Well, these kids may never be placed, except the pretty little girl because she's young. But these two boys…well, I don't know."

I was crushed. I was only five years old. Could I really be too old to get a family? Carole was only a few months younger than me. It made me even sadder for Eric because he was older than both of us. But if we were too old, then Wayne getting adopted was impossible, I thought.

I tried to get her crushing comments out of my head, but in midstream she said, "Well, one thing, whether they are placed or not, they will have great manners, because that old lady doesn't play." She could care less that we were sitting there listening. Everyone knew about Mama's strictness.

Life with my foster mother had its challenges. I always tried to rationalize why she was so strict. I contributed it to her age and the era in which she grew up. She was much older than the other mothers and fathers. Her punishments were so harsh at times. She was raised in an age where nonsense was not tolerated. When it came to ruling with a firm hand, Mama Thompson had no hard time doing just that. She beat you for anything. Sometimes I felt as if she enjoyed it. Don't get me wrong, I loved her with all my heart, but I often wondered if we were her biological children, would she have beaten us so severely?

Her biological son, Otis, was her pride and joy. Mama always made it a point to remind us that Otis was "high yella," meaning light-skinned, and had green eyes. More times than I cared to hear, she would remind me while combing my hair that she was glad Otis had, as she said, "good hair." Did she realize that what she said hurt my feelings? I wondered. At an early age I realized black people could be their own worst enemies when it came to prejudice, judging people for their skin color and even the texture of their hair.

Mama could be sweet, but little things set her off. I found myself on many occasions wondering why something so small would incur her wrath. On one particular day, I took a chest and slid it over to the television. At five years old, I was very inquisitive and smart, if I say so myself. I positioned the chest, fixed the rabbit ears, and turned on the TV. That one gesture resulted in me being sent to bed. I couldn't help but think, isn't this what five-year-olds do? Shouldn't this have been the time I was told, "Neil, you could have fallen off the chest and hurt yourself, and if you do it again, I will punish you"? However, that was not the case. It was five in the evening, and I was sent to bed after dinner.

I was hurt that Mama felt I deserved that. Although she didn't lay a hand on me, I could see the rage in her face. But I counted my blessings that she didn't whip me. I admit I was stubborn, or maybe stupid, because I always pushed the envelope. I remember I used to flick water on the bathroom mirror with my toothbrush, but after Mama found out who the culprit was, I never did that again.

Later on that week, I tried her patience once more. She served beans for dinner, and for whatever reason, I hated beans. So I wouldn't eat them. She didn't whip me because Ms. Nickinson, another social worker, was scheduled to come that day. But whether Ms. Nickinson was coming or not, I was sent to my room and told not to come out until she said so. I remember it so vividly, looking out the window and watching Mama say hello to Ms. Nickinson and seeing her explain why I wasn't in the yard playing with the other kids. When I didn't get beaten, I counted my blessings. But in the years to come, the extension cord would become a second skin.

CHAPTER ELEVEN

Being placed in foster care, I always tried to stay positive. So the thought of going to school that fall was my saving grace. But what continued to hurt was Mama's continued favoritism of Eric over me. I tried to come up with many reasons why Mama put Eric first, but I just couldn't. I soon realized age and time had nothing whatsoever to do with her treatment of me. She made it pretty clear that Eric was her favorite. Nevertheless, I remained upbeat and focused on the coming school year.

Spring and summer had come and gone. Mama and Ms. Kay started setting up appointments to get me vaccinated. That evening Ms. Kay came over with some vouchers for school clothes. When Ms. Kay took us shopping, I remember Mama buying things that were way too big for me. I picked out things, and she would say, "Let's put that back," and I couldn't understand why. Eventually I did get three new pairs of pants, three shirts, a black-and-brown necktie, another blazer, a pair of sneakers, and a pair of dress shoes.

When I got home, Mama told me to put my one bag of clothes away. Then she called Eric from outside and showed him three bags of new clothes and told him to put his new things away. She also said that when I said my prayers that night, I should thank God for my new clothes. In my mind, I thought what new clothes? How unfair that Eric got most of the clothes off my voucher, and for the life of me, I couldn't hold it in. I asked Mama, "Why did Eric get so much stuff?" Big mistake, as she took a shoe and hit me on the top of the head, and then she continued to take my pants down and spank my behind like there was no tomorrow. Then I was sent to bed.

As I lay there trying to hold back tears because I definitely didn't want her to hear me, I saw Eric putting his new clothes in the dresser. He didn't even look back or acknowledge me being upset. I realized then that Eric was selfish; if there wasn't something in it for him, then it didn't matter to him. I didn't want to start hating Eric because of Mama's actions, but it was made clear that day that Eric was for Eric.

Later that evening Mama asked me why I thought she beat me. I couldn't even answer; I was so hurt because I hadn't deserved it. So I just shook my head no. "I beat you because you shouldn't ever question Mama. I take very good care of you boys' clothes, and now that you have grown so much, you can fit Eric's. Eric has nice pants and shirts, and now they are going to look good on you."

But Eric's clothes were way too big for me, I kept thinking. But I didn't dare open my mouth. No sooner had that thought popped in my mind than she said, "The pants that are too long I will hem to fit you." That meant, yet again, I would get Eric's hand-me-downs. Whether it was a bike, a toy, or sharing my wagon, I never felt it was about me. The entire time I was in the Thompson household, although I knew Mama loved me and taught me so many valuable lessons, I never felt that comfort you get from someone who adores you.

Yes, I adored her because, after all, where would I be if I didn't have Mama? But that night I toughened up—Mama's favorite line. Often she would tell me to "quit acting like a stubborn baby and toughen up." And that night I did.

I asked God, "Please protect me and let me be happy. Also, God, please make sure Eric looks after me once we start school." Sometimes I worried because I didn't know if he would stand by me outside of the home. Usually when the neighborhood kids came over, he was pretty protective, so I felt I was in good hands. To Eric's credit, he always protected me. My doubting of Eric I contribute to Mama showing favoritism, which brought more insecurity. And within the blink of an eye, it was time to go to school.

CHAPTER TWELVE

The night before school started I asked Mama what I would wear on my first day of school. "I don't know, baby, but we can go pick something out." Mama could have her moments, and that night she seemed to focus on me, and that made me happy. "Neil, baby, what do you want to wear?" she asked. I looked at my clothes and decided to pick out my new brown pants and my red shirt. That night I had butterflies and tossed and turned all night. It was like the night before Christmas.

The next morning came fast; I couldn't believe that in a matter of a few hours I would be going to Goulding Elementary. Mama washed me and put on my clothes. Eric came in and bopped me on the top of the head and smiled. Mama immediately told him, "You behave, and make sure you look after your brother." That line eased my mind because I knew Eric would definitely obey Mama.

I thought about my birth mother, something I hadn't done in a while. I was sure she knew I was old enough to start school, and I wondered for a split second if she wondered if I was happy or if she regretted missing something so poignant in my life. I don't know; sometimes I couldn't help wondering if she thought about me at all.

Finally dressed, I admired how good I looked. I was officially a big boy. Mama called us kids in for breakfast, and I was so nervous I couldn't even eat. But Mama told me, "Neil, baby, you have to eat something." Mama made my first day of school so pleasant. She was attentive and made the day that I had anticipated very special. And I loved her for it.

But something was missing—Wayne. I knew he couldn't have forgotten me, because he was so excited for me. I started feeling sad, and at that moment he ran through the door. Mama yelled, as usual, "Boy, what are you doing here? You're going to be late for school!"

"Yes, ma'am, but I had to see Neil." He hugged me so tightly and kissed me on the cheek. He said quietly, "Neil, I love you, little brother; have a happy day." I smiled so hard I thought I would burst. I hugged him tight, and he looked around and saw Eric. "Eric, my man, you have a wonderful day too, and look out for your little brother."

Eric smiled and said, "I will." Eric also respected our older brother.

Mama just looked at Wayne and, in a manner fitting Mama, quipped, "Boy, you get going; you're going to be late." I knew she was a little irritated because Wayne made it a point to show me more attention than Eric. But I quickly shook that thought out of my mind because I didn't want to spoil my moment. Finally, I was going to Goulding Elementary.

As Mama, Eric, and I walked down the street toward the school, we started getting stares. At that point, it was clear that these were the neighbors I didn't see every day. I was suddenly reminded that I was in foster care. A couple of the older kids teased us about being unwanted. They made comments like, "The poor foster kids that live down the street with the mean old lady." You know, dumb stuff like that. But what made this scenario even worse was that their parents just stood there saying nothing; they just let their kids say mean things.

But Mama didn't take any mess. This was the time I appreciated Mama's smart mouth and intolerance for disrespectful people, no matter who they were. Mama took me and Eric by the hand and walked across the street toward them. She said, "I done told your kids in the past not to tease my boys, and to make matters worse, you're just standing there listening. Don't make me call the authorities, cuz I ain't gonna act a monkey like before. I'm getting too damn old for this mess." She pulled Eric and me away and sashayed back across the street. No one said a word. At five years old, I realized that day that kids emulate their parents. Although that minor distraction happened, I was still consumed with joy. I was both excited and anxious.

Entering the school, I was washed in the smell of cleaning products, new school clothes, and the scent of books. I will never forget it. It was one of my best memories growing up. I was hopeful that going to school would mean it wouldn't be long before some lucky family wanted me. I was no longer a baby but a big boy with so much to offer.

There were a couple of snickers from the other kids who knew we were foster kids. I heard one fifth grader say, "That's the old lady that has those kids who don't have a mama."

Another kid said, "Oh, I thought that was their grandmother."

"No, that's the mean old lady. I think she takes those kids in for the money." And then they laughed.

Nevertheless, I wanted to have a great day, so I shrugged it off. Mama obviously didn't hear them, because she would have been in their faces. God, I was glad she hadn't, because I didn't want my first day of school to be scarred any further because of someone's ignorance. But I would soon realize this was only the beginning of being known as a foster kid and being the target of jokes.

One bright spot was the vision of Ms. Dandridge, the principal, standing there and saying hello to the students and parents, hugging kids she'd known over the years. The presence of Mama was overwhelming because she was so respected. Ms. Dandridge walked over and hugged Mama and said, "Hello, Ms. Beatrice, it's good seeing you, and who is this handsome young man?" She hugged Eric and asked him, "Eric, did you have a good summer?"

Eric said, "Yes, ma'am," and smiled.

Mama said, "This is Neil Washington."

Suddenly I felt a pit in my stomach. It felt so impersonal. I wanted her to say, "This is my baby, Neil," but she didn't. Ms. Dandridge bent down and took my hand and said, "Well, Neil, it's nice to meet you. You are cute as a button," and hugged me the way she had Eric, and that made me feel wanted.

Ms. Dandridge looked at her paperwork and told Mama which rooms to take Eric and me to. At that moment I knew I had to let go of my attachment to Eric. I was going to be on my own without Mama, Wayne, and Eric. I was terrified. As Mama let go of Eric, before he walked away, she bent down and hugged him and told him to have a blessed day. Then she grabbed my hand and took me to my room. Mama bent down and hugged me too and said, "Don't worry, my baby, you will be just fine." I took a deep breath and thanked God that Mama had made me feel just as special as Eric, if only for a moment.

CHAPTER THIRTEEN

Mama Thompson wasn't an affectionate woman, so it was special when she showed a softer side of her. As Mama walked into the room to speak to my teacher, Ms. Nelson, I was consumed with a sense of sadness. I had never been away from Mama for a long period of time; she was my security blanket, and now she was leaving. Even though her strictness was hard to understand sometimes, I felt protected.

Ms. Nelson introduced herself and then said, "Neil, you sit here, if that's OK?" I smiled and sat down. Ms. Nelson told Mama, "He will be fine. Don't worry; I will take good care of him."

"Oh, honey, I know you will," Mama replied. "Neil, you be a good boy for Ms. Nelson, and I will see you in a few hours." Mama also mentioned to Ms. Nelson that I should do well in school because I was known to repeat everything I heard. I couldn't believe she told that to someone I met only a second ago. She continued with, "We call that boy 'Go.' I tell you, he would ride with the devil if given the chance."

Ms. Nelson smiled and said, "Well, let's say he's adventurous then." Mama bent down, and I hugged her and watched her walk away.

In a matter of minutes, the classroom filled up with my new class-mates. Ms. Nelson walked over to the students who were just standing around and led them to their seats; she talked to some of the parents and reassured all of us that today would be a special day. I was nervous yet excited to see what today had to offer. Once things got settled, Ms. Nelson pointed to each one of us to say our names.

Although I was extremely nervous, I knew one day I would become a leader. I just knew it. I felt good saying my name, "Neil Washington." It felt right. At that young age, I saw leadership in my future. This gift gave me brief insights into my life.

Ms. Nelson continued to explain what this year had in store for us. She expressed that we would be learning at a smooth pace and we would be expected to be polite and courteous to our classmates and to her. But what she expressed several times was that the sky was the limit, and we should always think positively and be proud of ourselves. I probably took that more personally than most, because I knew that being a foster kid meant I always had to encourage myself. That day not only did I realize that my name would be in a leadership role, but I also knew, at five years old, that I was going to be positive at all times, even when times got hard. I decided I would never let being a foster kid define who and what I was. I would never be less than anyone else, and I was going to be a sponge and soak up everything that God had for me. Tomorrow was a new day, but today was just the beginning.

Ms. Nelson told us to start getting our supplies together and that it was time to go home. Wow! I looked up, and my first day of school was about to come to an end. Today was so exciting. But before we left, Ms. Nelson had one-on-one time with all of us, which made the day even more special. She seemed impressed with me because I knew how to write my name; Wayne's help proved to be beneficial.

We were also given the dos and don'ts. Ms. Nelson expressed that she loved what she did; teaching was her passion, and she wanted us to reach for the sky. She was a soft-spoken woman, but I could tell she could be stern. But she also made it very clear that being mean and teasing anyone in class would get you punished. Although her words went over almost everyone's heads, she made it clear that she would be fair but would not tolerate nonsense in her classroom. My first day of school was one of the most memorable and poignant times in my life. I felt like a normal kid, as if I had a real family. I felt happy and, most of all, content. I didn't feel as if I was a foster kid. These feelings would be hard to fathom if you didn't grow up in foster care, praying you'd fit in.

Finally Ms. Nelson walked us into the hall, lining us up against the wall to wait for someone to come get us. The last thing she said was, "Practice your name, and I can't wait to see your smiling faces tomorrow." She hugged every one of us. I looked up, and to my surprise, there was Wayne. I kept thinking, what is he doing here? He should be in school.

He walked over and asked me, "How was your day, baby brother?" I hugged him and told him it was fun, and that pleased him. But he asked me something that day that would haunt me the rest of my life. He asked me, "Did anybody tease you about being a foster kid?"

I told him no. And thankfully no one had said a thing—besides the incident that happened earlier. I knew if I didn't have this gift, I wouldn't understand the impact of kids teasing us about being foster kids. But Wayne had endured this pain for a long time, and he didn't want me to feel those emotions. Walking home, Wayne was pretty quiet. He held onto my hand and reached over to pick up my book bag. Wayne's behavior made me feel unsettled. I asked him if we could play when we got home, and he said, really softly, "I doubt it; we will see."

Standing at the screen door was Mama with a shoe. I didn't understand it, or maybe I didn't want to understand it. After all, my day was great; at least that's what I thought, so I prayed she was simply swatting a fly. She yelled, "Wayne, get your ass up here now!" He let go of my hand and tried to run past her.

Yes, Mama was up in age, but we could never run from her. And before I could tell her how wonderful my day was, she hit Wayne in his back with her shoe. He didn't scream or even flinch. She continued whaling on him as I stood there in disbelief, my book bag in my hands and Carole looking out the window. The other kids weren't home from school yet. I was terrified. Yes, it was selfish, but I stood there thinking, how did such a wonderful day end so horribly? Finally Mama realized a couple of the neighbors were staring, so she stopped beating Wayne. She yelled to me, "Neil, get in there, boy, and change your clothes." I walked past her, and she grabbed my book bag. I couldn't explain why Mama attacked Wayne, but I was terrified.

I heard Mama tell Wayne that she didn't take him in to have him lie to her. I thought, there she goes, those words that cut us to our cores. She never once told us that she took us in because she loved, cared, or enjoyed having us; it was always that we should be forever grateful. And trust me, we were. We knew Mama had a wonderful heart, although sometimes we couldn't see it from her demeanor. But I thanked God she took me, because, after all, where would I be? I wished she could understand our gratitude.

I took off my pants slowly, because I didn't want to go back into the front room. Besides, Mama could be so unpredictable. She could tell us to come back out yet accuse us of being nosey, so I held off until I felt it was safe.

Taking my life in my own little hands, I finally walked out. I noticed a police officer and Wayne's social worker, Mr. Beal, sitting in the front room. Mr. Beal mentioned to Mama that Wayne did make it to his first day of school, but for some reason he had left early, because Officer Jones had noticed him wandering around downtown around ten o'clock that morning. The officer said he pulled next to Wayne and asked him why he wasn't at school. He could tell Wayne was his son's age. Wayne had only replied that he left early. Officer Jones said because Wayne was so polite, his heart went out to him. He didn't want to make Wayne feel that he was in trouble but wanted him to know he actually had a friend in Officer Jones.

Nevertheless, he couldn't overlook the fact that this kid was skipping school. Wayne volunteered the information that he was in foster care and gave Mr. Beal's name. I'm sure he was hoping and praying Mr. Beal would add some type of buffer for Mama. Now it all made sense why Wayne had picked me up today. Mr. Beal tried to calm the situation because Mama was so agitated. Officer Jones was very caring, considering Wayne was another Pensacola black teenager in trouble. He told Mama, "Well, Ms. Thompson, this young man isn't the first young man today who was caught skipping school, so try and calm down." I don't think she even heard him. I don't think Mama realized we had bad days.

Mr. Beal asked Wayne, "Son, why did you skip class today?" Wayne hesitated as Eric and the other kids were starting to come home from school. Wayne finally answered in his hurt and shaking voice. He told Officer Jones and Mr. Beal that when the kids who didn't live in the neighborhood realized he was in the Thompson household, they had started making fun of him because he was in foster care.

CHAPTER FOURTEEN

So going into high school was like Wayne's first day of school all over again. I kept praying Mama would walk up to him and say, "Well, son, it's OK, and I'm so proud of you." But very, very rarely was Mama comforting. Her demeanor was passionless, unless it was a passionate ass whupping. Mr. Beal and Officer Jones both interjected and told Wayne that he would have to press on and ignore the disappointment of today. They encouraged him to look at the big picture and told him that he was a smart young man and had the rest of his life to show these kids what he was made of. And although their words were meaningful and inspirational, you can't see anything farther than the nose on your face when you are being teased unmercifully.

I listened to both of them encouraging Wayne. I was happy that they cared, but I was scared because I knew eventually I would become a target too. I could see out of the corner of my eye that Mama was tapping her foot. I wanted to walk over to this woman and shake her. I wanted to tell her that although I was grateful she didn't leave me in Escambia Hospital, we needed more than a roof over our heads.

Wayne listened intently, and I could tell he was beginning to feel better having two people care so much about him. Mr. Beal and Officer Jones asked Mama if they could speak to Wayne alone, and with no fight, she said, "Do what ya want with that boy."

They took Wayne outside, and Mama started to get us dinner. She had a meatloaf in the refrigerator. She put it in the oven, and finally showing some normalcy, she started asking us how our day was. We all sat down and filled her in, and I started to feel less agitated and scared. Carole came out and finally looked at the papers scattered on the table. She asked me, "Neil, can I write with your pencil?" I felt like an older brother as I helped her. I finally felt as if this horrid day was going to be OK.

After half an hour, Wayne, Mr. Beal, and Officer Jones returned. Mr. Beal was so attentive. Mama was beginning to cool down and asked them if they wanted some sweet tea. In the meantime, Officer Jones said he would love to follow up on Wayne and go to the school and make sure they talked to some of the staff to inform them of this incident today.

I looked at Wayne and could tell his emotions were mixed. I'm sure he felt some type of relief, but who wanted to be a tattletale, especially a tattletale in foster care? Officer Jones assured Wayne that he wouldn't mention him personally, and I could see a look of relief cross Wayne's face.

Mama said, "I tell this boy all the time that he is smart. He just gotta let this nonsense roll off his back." Mama started getting us cleaned up for dinner and helped us finish our homework. Although the day definitely didn't end the way I had hoped, I was still excited for tomorrow. Eventually Mr. Beal and Officer Jones left, and I prayed Mama wouldn't revert back to beating Wayne, and thankfully she didn't. She sat Wayne down and told him that he was a foster child and of course there were stupid kids that wouldn't understand his situation, but he couldn't let that stop him from going to school. Finally she asked me, "Neil, baby, how was your day?" I finally gave the answer that I wanted to give all day. I told her that I had fun and I liked school.

And like that, the day was now behind us. I said my prayers and asked God to help Wayne. I was so sad for him, yet I was excited for myself. I didn't know how to feel at this point, but what I did know was I hated to see the most important person in my life in so much pain. "God, please let Wayne have a great day tomorrow and all those mean kids leave him alone, AMEN." And before I could roll over, it was morning.

CHAPTER FIFTEEN

The next morning we all got ready for school. When I saw Eric check his book bag, I did the same; I always followed Eric. Mama called us to eat breakfast. Mama asked Wayne to say grace. Wayne grabbed my hand so tightly it hurt. He said softly, "God, thank you for this food that Mama prepared this morning. God, please let us have a wonderful day, and please let me be all right, amen." I wanted to be happy going to my second day of school, but I couldn't. I shouldn't have understood this pain of Wayne's, but I did.

We were about to finish breakfast when there was a knock at the door. "Hey, baby, how are you this morning?" said Mama.

It was Tommy's dad, Mr. Jamison. "Good morning, Ms. Beatrice. Tommy told me what happened yesterday, and I was hoping to lend whatever hand I can."

"Well, Jimmy, I don't know what you can do, but that boy is going to school regardless. He's getting ready now." I couldn't help but think why can't Mama shut up?

Mr. Jamison said, "Well, would it be possible to see him and maybe take him and Tommy to school today?" For the first time in twenty-four hours, I could see some joy in Wayne's face. He looked at Mr. Jamison and smiled. "Hello, son, how are you today?" said Mr. Jamison.

"I'm good, Mr. Jamison. Wazzup, Tommy?" I could tell Tommy was uncomfortable, because he wasn't himself. Nevertheless, everyone tried to act normal. I remember Mr. Jamison slapping me five for going to school. That was why I loved him; he was so caring. On the days he took Wayne for a haircut, he would bring everyone something small to say he thought of us too. Ms. Joyce, Tommy's mom, was the same; she would often send over cookies or brownies. I prayed all the time that they wanted to adopt me, but they already had Tommy.

"Hey, young man, it's going to be a better day today; I thought you might want to ride with Tommy," said Mr. Jamison.

Wayne immediately looked at Mama, and she nodded yes. But before Mr. Jamison and Wayne could get out the door Mama said, "Jimmy, thanks, but don't go spoiling this boy. He gotta toughen up and ride the bus."

"Yes, ma'am, Ms. Beatrice, but just for today..."

I ran over to Wayne and told him I loved him. I looked into his eyes and I didn't see the boy I had grown to love who adored me. His eyes were blank, and his face was sad. He whispered, "I love you, Neil. Always remember that."

Mama yelled out the door, "Wayne, when you get home, don't forget to start your chores." What she should have said was, "Have a good day, be careful, stay calm, and I'm here for you, son." I was grateful for Mr. Jamison and Tommy.

Time moved quickly, and it was time for Eric and me to put on our school clothes. I prayed to God that Wayne would have a great day. I loved Wayne. He was my brother, and I adored him. Our connection didn't seem real; it was uncanny to say the least.

Goulding Elementary wasn't far from the house, so we strolled along quietly; no one really said anything. I wanted to be happy, but I felt guilty because I knew Wayne was sad and his day uncertain. Eric asked Mama if she wanted to see where his room was. I kept thinking, she dropped you off twenty-four hours ago; did your room change? I loved Eric, but it was always about him, even as a little boy. Being cursed with this gift, I remembered Eric's first day of school; Mama made him cupcakes and a special dinner. I didn't want to be sad because Mama made a difference between me and Eric, because if I did, then I would be sad a lot. Mama told me, "Neil, when you get out of school, you wait for me." I could see my teacher, Ms. Nelson. She remembered my name, and that made me feel on top of the world.

"Good morning, Neil. How are you, dear?" she said. I couldn't help myself, and I ran over and hugged her. She continued to ask me questions. "How did you spend the evening of your first day of school?" And I thought, God, if she only knew.

Mama chirped in and said, "He was fine. We did his homework. I hope he didn't forget anything, because that boy would lose his head if it wasn't attached."

"No, ma'am, the kids only had in their book bags what I placed in there personally, so I'm sure he did everything he was supposed to do." It was sad that a lady I just met had more confidence in me than Mama.

"Neil, don't you forget to wait here, and have a nice day, baby." I hugged her; I did love Mama. I looked back and noticed Carole had her head down. So I went back to hug her, and she slapped my face. I was stunned, yet not surprised, because Carole had an evil streak that was hard to overlook at times. Mama hauled off and slapped her face, and I smiled. This was the early seventies, so child abuse was unheard of; back then it was simply called discipline.

Ms. Nelson looked the other way and grabbed my hand and said, "C'mon, Neil, let's see what this wonderful day has for us." I was so excited to leave Mama, Carole, the crying babies, Eric, and even Wayne's issues behind for now. I was grabbing onto happiness, if only for a few hours. Today Ms. Nelson wanted to get to know us all better. So she went around the room and asked our favorite color, and raising my hand high, I let everyone know that red was my favorite color. She also asked what we did on summer vacations. My heart skipped a beat; this was another time, being placed in foster care, when I wanted to disappear. Generally on weekends we played in the yard, and on Sundays we went to church.

I remember this kid Joey stood up and said his dad, his brother, and his uncle Willy went fishing all summer, and then the floodgates opened and most everyone wanted to stand up and tell how their summers were spent. I looked at Ms. Nelson, and I could tell she sensed something. So she said, "Well, you all sound like you had a wonderful summer and fulfilling weekends, but sometimes it's nice to sit home, drink some lemonade, play around in your yard, and enjoy your family." She looked at me and winked, and I knew God was looking down on me.

However, things did change the following year. Mama had a friend in Alabama who had a farm, and we would go there for two weeks in the summers, so that was the last time I felt ashamed of my summer. Mama also started taking us on picnics, beach trips, and to parties, mostly with the church. There were also times we would venture out to the mall. As foster kids, we weren't cooped up like prisoners, at least not in the Thompson household. Even though Mama was older, she did try and entertain us the best she could.

Suddenly thoughts of Wayne started to pop into my head, and I wondered if he was going to be outside waiting for me. God, I hope not, I thought. As Ms. Nelson gave us instructions for our second day of homework, I couldn't help but notice some of the kids getting excited about someone picking them up. Some of them were talking about their moms and, in some cases, dads. I sat there, saddened that my mom didn't even know me. I looked toward the sky and asked silently, why can't I be a normal little boy? Why do I have to suffer with this gift, and most of all, why couldn't I have been born to a mother that wanted to know the little boy that I am and the man that I pray to become?

But if God was listening, he wasn't answering right then. As quickly as the day began, it was over. I grabbed my book bag and walked toward the door with the uncertainty of what tonight would offer. I prayed that today would be better than yesterday. Ms. Nelson hugged every last one of us and told us to make sure to do our homework. I held my breath, praying Wayne wasn't there. Thank God it was Mama.

"Neil, baby, how was your day? Did you have a good day, son?" She said "son," and that warmed my heart. Sometimes as foster kids all we yearn to hear is "son" or "daughter." You can't imagine how heartfelt that longing was.

I smiled brightly and said, "Good, Mama. I had fun." A day late, but today it was welcomed. Carole was different too; she looked at me and said, "Neil, can we play?" Obviously she had missed me too. Mama didn't even yell. Sometimes our horsing around got on her nerves, but for whatever reason, she seemed content right now. When we arrived home, I ran to my room and changed my clothes. I could see Mama going through my bag. She told me and Carole to go outside to play for a while, and she was going to start dinner.

A couple of hours later, Eric came walking down the street. I could see him talking and playing around with the neighborhood kids. I felt a little jealous because it was obvious he was now making new friends.

Wayne was also coming home, a little later than normal. He walked over to me and Carole and hugged us. He asked me, "How was your day, baby brother?"

I smiled and said, "Good." I wanted to ask him the same question but didn't. He saw Eric coming and waited to hug him too. He was the big brother other kids dreamed of. Eric asked him the question I didn't know how to ask. Eric just blurted it out. "Did you get in trouble today?"

Wayne smiled and said, "Nope, I didn't, Eric." Wayne walked toward the stairs.

Mama came out and said, "Young man, was you on your best behavior today?"

Wayne said softly, "Yes, ma'am."

"Thank you, Lord. No tomfoolery like yesterday," she said.

Wayne looked at her and smiled and said, "No, ma'am, everything was OK." Tomfoolery was not Wayne's issue; it was surviving being a target of kids who rubbed it in his face that he didn't belong because he was a foster kid.

I noticed a car coming down the street that I didn't recognize. It was Officer Jones in his own vehicle. He had come to check on Wayne, and I couldn't believe my eyes. Not too often would people who weren't getting paid come to follow up on us. Officer Jones was genuinely concerned. Wayne came to the door, and Officer Jones said, "Hey, son, how was your day today? Did you make out OK?"

"Yes, sir, it was better." Mama came to the door and asked him to come in, and like that, they all disappeared inside.

CHAPTER SIXTEEN

Carole, Eric, and I stayed outside. I looked up, and there was Mr. Jamison and Wayne's social worker, Mr. Beal. It didn't make sense. Mr. Jamison gave all of us new notebooks with pencils. "Ms. Beatrice," he called, "just a couple of things for the kids. I hope you don't mind."

"Come in here, Jimmy. No, I don't mind. Every little bit helps." I looked at Mama, and she seemed somewhat confused herself. However, she remained calm. She told us to stay in the yard and yelled across the street to Ms. Clara, asking, "Can you keep an eye out for these kids?" And before I could blink, they all disappeared inside. Eric and I did our best to hear what was going on. We played closer to the house and even pressed our luck and ran on the porch from time to time, knowing if Mama was aware of this our little asses would regret it. I sat down on a stump; I couldn't hear anything.

But without warning, I could see myself as an adult. I could see men and women in uniform saying things like, "Hey, Sergeant, good looking out." I could see classmates from a school named Tate. I could see someone named Mr. Boyd, someone from some ranch who was knowledgeable about my future and whom I trusted. I couldn't explain it right then, but he was a comfort somehow. I saw a small-statured, petite, beautiful woman who made my heart melt and whom I loved. I saw a little girl with sandals smiling and hugging me; maybe it was someone from school telling me she was a good girl all day. It wasn't Carole, but she was adorable.

She took my breath away, yet I didn't know her pretty face. I saw a young man thanking me for fighting for him and not letting him become a statistic like me. Obviously he was a soldier because he had a uniform on. I couldn't put a name to his face, but somehow he was special to me. I saw a much older gentleman telling me that I had made him look like he did when he was young, and then he laughed. He followed that with, "Young man, I'm glad you are home safe."

I saw an older lady, small in stature, thanking me for everything I had done. She continued to tell me that I was a blessing to her and she loved me and forgiveness was important. She continued to look at me and said, "You turned out to be a wonderful young man, and thanks for all your help. You've been a true blessing to me." I didn't know who she was. There were so many people telling me thank you that I didn't know. I tried my best to recognize these people, but I couldn't.

Everything was blurred and didn't make sense; however, what did make sense? I saw Wayne telling me, "Thank you, little brother. I always felt loved with you, and I will be by your side always. I will never leave you, Neil, ever." And just like that I was the little boy waiting outside, scared. I prayed to God that everything was OK, but call it intuition and not a gift—I felt lost. Somehow I knew things would never be the same.

CHAPTER SEVENTEEN

I sat there confused and scared. Carole walked over and yelled in my face. "Neil, help!" Carole's shoe had gotten stuck in a small hole. Eric walked over and helped her. "Neil, did you hear that?" Eric said. Suddenly I could hear Mama yelling. All of a sudden we saw Wayne burst out of the door and Officer Jones on his heels chasing him. I didn't know what to do, so I sat there in a daze. Officer Jones ran behind Wayne. Mr. Beal came to the door and also started to run down the street. I could hear Mama yelling, "Boy, get your ass back here!" I could see Officer Jones grabbing Wayne by the back of the neck. Officer Jones and Mr. Beal huddled around Wayne and hugged him. Mama continued screaming at the top of her lungs. I knew whatever happened today would change my life forever.

Mama screamed for Eric, Carole, and me to get in the house. She sent us to our bedrooms. Eric asked me, "Neil, what do you think happened?" I sat on the edge of the bed shaking my head. I didn't know. But whatever it was—it was really bad.

I looked out my bedroom window, and I could see the three of them walking up the sidewalk. I could also see the neighbors gathering outside, and that infuriated Mama. I heard her say, "People so damn nosey." But what she failed to realize was that Wayne, a police officer, and a social worker had been running down the street, with her screaming at the top of her lungs.

Officer Jones called Mama outside while Mr. Beal took Wayne around to the backyard. The windows were open, so Eric and I could hear what was being said. Thank God! "Ms. Thompson," said Officer Jones, "I understand your concerns, and I understand why you are so upset, but yelling, screaming, and beating that young man will not resolve this situation."

I thought with a police officer telling Mama those words that she would be scared, as we were. But no one told Mama how to correct her kids. Mama wasn't scared of anything but Jesus Christ; she said that all the time. She walked closer to Officer Jones and said, "Look here, Officer, I sacrifice for these kids, and having this boy disrespect me will not be tolerated in my household."

Officer Jones just stood there saying nothing. I guess he felt like the rest of us kids; he had no voice with this old lady. "Well, I understand you are mad, ma'am, but we cannot stand here and let you put hands on this young man; it's the law." No one said anything.

Wayne and Mr. Beal walked from around the house. Mr. Beal said, "Ms. Thompson, I've talked to Wayne, and I'm hoping we can go inside and talk in private without the neighbors."

I remember hearing a knock at the door, and it was Ms. Clara from across the street. She came into the bedroom and said, "C'mon, boys, get your book bags and your pajamas." My first thought was, are we going to live with Ms. Clara now?

Everything seemed so uncertain at this point. I was so scared I started to shake. But I gathered up my things. I saw Eric getting his stuff together and Ms. Clara getting Carole. Mama was holding one of the babies and told Ms. Clara she shouldn't be long. She told Ms. Clara to pull out the leftovers.

"Beatrice, don't you worry. I have plenty of food for these kids; you take care of yourself, and don't worry." Mama managed a smile.

Living with Wayne would forever change that night. Once we got to Ms. Clara's house, we continued to play for a while with Ms. Clara's children, Cheryl and Wilson. Both of them were Wayne's friends. I heard Ms. Clara ask them to "make the boys feel comfortable." Ms. Clara had Carole in the kitchen with her, letting her put forks on the table. I sat there, still stunned and confused. I knew that my life would never, ever be the same.

I overheard Ms. Clara ask Wilson, "So what do you think will happen to Wayne?"

"Mama, I don't know."

"Neil, are you ready to eat some dinner?" Cheryl asked. I shook my head no. "C'mon, Neil, you will grow up strong, so you have to eat a little something." She grabbed my hand and walked toward the kitchen. Eric and Carole were already seated.

Ms. Clara began to say grace. "Thank you for this food and our lovely company tonight...well...they're not company they're family, so thank you, Lord, for our family. And Lord, please protect the Thompson household and make everything all right. Amen." And in unison we all said, "Amen."

CHAPTER EIGHTEEN

During dinner, Eric asked Ms. Clara, "Do you know what happened today, Ms. Clara?"

"Now, young man, that is for your mama to tell you. Besides, honey, I really don't know." Later, Ms. Clara was impressed that we took our plates to the sink without being asked. I would learn to appreciate Mama for making me so responsible at such a young age. What she taught me would forever live on, and I would become a better man for it.

Ms. Clara asked Cheryl and Wilson to help get us cleaned up. "Neil, do you like school?" Cheryl asked. I nodded my head yes, but I wanted to tell her the only thing I remembered about my first days of school was pure disappointment. Police officers and social workers, Mama beating and screaming at Wayne—so, no, my memory of school was pure torture.

Nevertheless, I continued to pretend that everything was OK. Well, I guess for the most part I did have a great day at school; it was coming home that terrified me. I pretended a lot as a foster child. I pretended I was OK living with someone other than my parents, that I was tough when kids teased me about being a foster kid, and that it was my biological family's loss because they didn't want me. I realized pretending was my survival mechanism. There were days when I pretended that I had a mother who adored the little boy that I was. Or I pretended potential parents didn't move on to the next kid because of my dark skin and that I finally got adopted.

I pretended a lot while in foster care.

Once settled, we were allowed to watch TV. That was a big deal to us, because generally the only time we got to watch TV was Saturday cartoons or when Mama watched the evening news. I saw some of the porch lights come on. I looked across the street, and now there was another car besides Officer Jones's and Mr. Beal's cars. I didn't recognize it. I heard the phone ring, and I heard Ms. Clara tell Cheryl and Wilson to "get the boys ready to go home." Ms. Clara carried Carole, who had fallen asleep. I prayed while gathering my things that when I went home everything would be calm and Mama wouldn't be upset.

Standing in the yard were Officer Jones, Mr. Beal, and now another man I didn't know. I found out later that his name was Mr. Harlem, and he was also from social services. They were standing in the yard. Mama walked out, and they all shook hands. I could see Wayne coming out with a suitcase. I could see Wayne look toward us and quickly walk past Mama. When we got to the yard, Mama said, "Well, you all might as well know that Wayne is going to live somewhere else for now." I was stunned, hurt, and in disbelief. I'd been with Wayne as long as I'd been with Mama. I started to cry.

Wayne walked over and picked me up and said, "Neil, it's OK, little brother. Please be a big boy, and don't cry." But I couldn't help it. After all, Wayne and I had a connection that no one else did. Mama walked over and told everyone that it was best they leave. I overheard her saying, "Cuz this boy will cry all night." I looked at Wayne and ran toward him. He picked me up and kissed both Eric and me, and although Carole was asleep in Ms. Clara's arms, he kissed her.

Cheryl and Wilson just stood there in disbelief. I heard Wilson ask Wayne, "Will you be in school tomorrow?" Wayne shook his head no.

Ms. Clara walked over and handed Carole to Mama and then walked toward Wayne and hugged him tight.

She told him she would be praying for him and to please come see her when he came back home. I was now crying uncontrollably, and Mama told Eric to take me in the house. But Ms. Clara pulled me by the hand and said in the most comforting voice, "Neil, be a big boy; I'm sure Wayne is going to spend the night somewhere while everyone calms down." She took me and Eric to our bedrooms and told us to lie down until Mama came in. I remember crying myself to sleep.

The next morning I woke up thinking that Wayne would be back home by now. But when I got up, it seemed eerily quiet. The babies weren't fussy, and Eric was already outside playing. And then it hit me that today was Saturday, and I was thankful. Mama came over and gave me a hug. That was out of character for her, but I welcomed it. She told me to go brush my teeth and put on my play clothes and that she was cooking breakfast and would call Eric and me in when she was done. Carole was sitting in front of the TV watching cartoons. I didn't dare ask about Wayne, but I wanted some answers.

Finally she called us in to eat. Ms. Clara yelled from across the street, "Good morning, Beatrice. How are you this morning?"

"Oh, I'm blessed, Clara. I'm blessed after all this nonsense. Come over, Clara, around noon, and we'll have some tea. I want to thank you for helping me and the kids yesterday, and I will fill you in." And that was music to my ears. Hopefully I could get some answers about Wayne.

"Beatrice, no thanks needed, but I will see you then." Ms. Clara was genuinely concerned about us. About an hour later, Ms. Clara knocked on the door. I ran over and hugged her so tight; she was truly comfort to my little heart.

CHAPTER NINETEEN

As Ms. Clara got settled, she said, "Beatrice, how are you? You know the kids and I have been praying for you and Wayne."

I heard Mama say, "Well, Clara, you don't have to continue praying for me, cuz that boy is the one who's gonna need your prayers. I officially washed my hands of that boy." I couldn't believe my ears. That was another disadvantage to being in foster care: if someone didn't want us, they traded us in like a used car.

Ms. Clara looked stunned. "Whatcha mean, Beatrice?"

"I told that cop and those social workers to take him. I have sacrificed for that boy, and he turned out like this."

Ms. Clara said, "Do you mean Wayne isn't coming home?"

"Yes, that boy ain't coming back here, Clara. I have had enough of his shenanigans. All the kids I done had in this house, I've never had anyone of them bring cops to my house or cause me the trouble that boy did."

From the look on Ms. Clara's face, we both felt the same emotion—sadness. I couldn't believe my ears; I couldn't imagine my life without Wayne. Mama continued, "I told them social workers to put him in another foster home, and God bless whoever takes that kid. He's too weak for the Thompson household."

"What would make you say such a thing, Beatrice?"

Mama looked at Ms. Clara with a demeanor that displayed a lot of attitude and replied, "I said such a thing, Clara, because that boy needs to get a tough skin. If he is going to run or fight every time some kid calls him a throwaway or teases him for being in foster care, he will be running the rest of his life. Hell, the reality is, he *is* in foster care, and he needs to accept it. I ain't never had no cops or social workers question how I raise these kids. I'll be damned if I'm gonna have it now. Telling me I need to be more patient my ass."

Ms. Clara continued with, "So where is he going to go, Beatrice? Are you sure you want to do this?"

"You damn right I want to do this." Mama didn't appreciate Ms. Clara questioning her decision. Ms. Clara stood there waiting for another answer, but to no avail. I knew from that point on Mama and Ms. Clara's friendship was never going to be the same.

"All I know, Clara, is this. He's up in age, so they mentioned that boys' ranch in Gonzales, and that's fine by me. I have too much going on with these other kids to be distracted."

Ms. Clara looked disgusted, but she didn't say anything. But before she totally clammed up, she said, "Well, Beatrice, I know it has got to be hard growing up like these kids. My kids tell me all the time what goes on at school, and it just saddens me."

For a moment I thought Mama was going to say something that showed she loved Wayne, but without conscience, she said, "Well, that boy was growing so fast that he was eating me out of house and home, so it's probably for the best."

Ms. Clara stood there in disbelief. It was obvious to her that nothing was going to change Mama's mind, so she calmly gulped the last of her tea and said, "Well, I will continue to keep you, the kids, and especially Wayne in my prayers. I'll be seeing you at church tomorrow."

I kept praying that once things calmed down Mama would miss Wayne and want him back. I felt uneasy that entire day. I wanted to play with Carole and Eric, but I couldn't. I just lay in bed. It was getting late, and I knew Wayne wasn't home.

CHAPTER TWENTY

We sat down for dinner. Mama said grace and finally explained that Wayne would not be returning. She said Wayne didn't follow the rules and she was too old to deal with someone disrespecting her. And before I could digest this, she said, "I don't want to hear any grumbling, crying, or questions, because what's done is done." I was brokenhearted! Wayne wasn't coming home. And I didn't want to eat anymore. So I pushed my green beans and pot roast around the plate numerous times, and that got Mama's attention.

"Neil, if you ain't gonna eat that food, then put your plate in the Frigidaire." And with an "excuse me," I did just that. That night I missed my brother terribly. There was so much I depended on Wayne for. I would call Wayne to help me color, help in the bathroom, and most of all, I called him for affection—something that was missing in the Thompson household. I prayed that he would come back for me one day.

The next morning when I woke up, I ran to Wayne's room. There was still no Wayne, yet I was still hopeful. I noticed Mr. Beal and Officer Jones pulling up. I ran over to them and asked, "Where is Wayne?"

Mr. Beal picked me up and hugged me tight. "Hello, Neil." I turned around, and now Mr. Jamison was pulling up. "Neil, where is Mama Thompson?" Mr. Jamison asked. I pointed to the house; Mr. Jamison was really distant.

I knew something really bad had happened, because social workers very rarely came to our house on the weekends, unless it was planned.

Ms. Joyce and Ms. Clara were talking and walking toward the house. Ms. Clara told us to go over to her house, and both of them went inside to get the babies.

The outcome that morning was overwhelming. I never imagined that what was being discussed would change my life forever. I learned that Wayne had run away from the boys' home last night and hung himself. A factory employee had forgotten his lunch box on Friday and went to get it. When he arrived, he saw a young boy hanging from a beam. I overheard Mr. Clark, one of the neighbors, saying he had worked down at the factory for over thirty years and had never witnessed grown men being so overcome by grief. The gentleman who found Wayne ran over and cut his lifeless body down and attempted CPR, but he realized it was pointless. He concluded Wayne must have been there a long time, because his body was already cold. He wrapped Wayne up with a blanket and gathered up what was left behind. Wayne had left a note and some of his drawings.

His note was left to a few people. He told his mother he loved her but would never forgive her for separating him from the little brother who adored him and for not coming back for them. He continued, telling her that he had waited and prayed every day that she would come back for them. He also prayed in his death that she would do the right thing and get his little brother out of foster care. He thanked Tommy for his undying friendship and Mr. and Mrs. Jamison for being the parents that he never had.

He thanked Mr. Beal and Officer Jones for their support in the last few weeks, especially Mr. Beal for being a wonderful social worker over the years. Finally, in a message to Mama, he expressed to her that he never felt loved by her and that he felt he was more of a burden. He tried to relay to Mama that she thought love was placing a roof over your head and a hot meal in your stomach, but it was so much more than that. And with his death, he prayed she would soften and show more affection with the others. However, he thanked her for doing her best.

CHAPTER TWENTY-ONE

But what really broke my heart was the fact that he wrote a letter to me. Although he knew I wouldn't be able to understand it, he prayed that the Jamisons would relay the message once I got older. The letter started off with, "Neil, I pray one day you will receive this or at least be told what I have written to you…"

Neil, I'm sorry I had to leave you, but thank you for making me feel wanted and special no matter how my day was going. You were not the biological brother that I lost in foster care, but you were the little brother that always knew when I was hurting. I know your struggles, and I pray you will press on, little brother, once you get older, and don't be a statistic like me; you are better than that. I will always do my best to watch over you. I love you and Tommy; you are my brothers in life and death. I will also continue to look over my biological brother. Neil, call me what you want when you are older and you can understand this, but I couldn't take anymore. I'm sorry. Some people would call me a coward. I was taught if you don't want something you give it away or you do what you know is best, and I don't know what is best, so I did what is best for me. Mr. and Mrs. Jamison, Tommy, and Neil, I'm sorry, and I love you all. Neil, I will always be by your side; I will never leave you again. Ms. Thompson, thank you for doing your best.

And that was the end of his letter.

Of course I knew what he said; my gift allowed me that. I was devastated; I would forever hold Wayne in my heart. My gift also allowed me to see the reactions of everyone else. And I could see that Wayne had pretty much embarrassed Mama, and she wasn't about to go out grace-fully. She put on an even, hardened stance and said, "Well, if the only thing he could appreciate about me was I gave him a meal and a roof over his head, I'm glad I made my decision. God knew he was ungrate-ful." Gasps filled the room at her insensitive comment. For the first time in her life, I think she knew she was out of line. But did she clean it up? Absolutely not, because that was Mama.

I was devastated. The rest of the day I remember crying. Mama thought I had a fever, and although she took my temperature several times, she didn't understand why I continued crying. I was crying because the person who loved me the most was gone.

Over the next few days, I remember it was hectic at home. Although this had happened, we still went to church, and the whole church was overwhelmed with sadness. Members sent over food and offered to take some of us so Mama could relax. But what they didn't know was Mama *was* relaxed. I won't say that Mama was happy about Wayne, but she sure didn't seem sad either.

Later that day Mama, Mr. Beal, and the Jamisons went back to meet with the pastor to discuss Wayne's memorial. I remember it being so painful; I just checked out. But that was my way of dealing with it. From that day on, I went into survival mode. Later on in life I guess it did affect me, but you build a wall when you have no one else—at least I did. Some people called it hardened, but I called it survival. What I did remember was Wayne had a closed casket because of the trauma to his neck. But I was glad I didn't see my brother like that; I wanted to remember him the way he was, always with love in his eyes for me.

Wayne's neighborhood friends and their families were at the memo-rial. There were the Jamisons, of course, and Tommy, Ms. Clara, Wilson,

Cheryl, and some of the social workers from Pensacola's children's services, and more classmates came out than I expected. And to my surprise, caring strangers who had heard and just wanted to pay their respects were there as well. I prayed, asking why couldn't Wayne have seen how many people loved him instead of the few that had teased him? It may have made a difference if Wayne could have seen this in life, but that's what happens; we show people we care long after they're gone, and that's sad.

I kept thinking, what would his family say if they knew about Wayne's death? But what I didn't know was that his family had been notified. The social worker had contacted his biological mother, and she had said, "Do what you want with him; we don't have any money," and that was it. She also told them she had no idea where his little brother was, because she had never tried to see him either after she placed him. At that point I cried for Wayne. I cried about him, I cried because he was gone, but most of all, I cried for me. I missed him.

CHAPTER TWENTY-TWO

After Wayne's death, it was pretty clear that I was now alone. After a few days, Eric resumed being Eric. He would go outside and play all day. I often wondered if he missed Wayne. He never mentioned him or that he missed him. After a few more days, I guess Mama realized she should address the issue. Mama sat us all down and told us that Wayne didn't want to face his problems. "Wayne now has to deal with the Lord, because what Wayne did was not what the Lord would want him to do. What Wayne did was take the coward's way out." I was hurt by her insensitive words. How could she be so negative, knowing that Wayne was no longer coming home and she would never get another opportunity to say she loved him?

But that was Mama, feisty, sometimes caring, and most times mean. Ms. Jamison knocked on the door. We all jumped up to hug her. She asked Mama how she was and did she need anything? Mama told her no, that everything was OK, and she was trying to explain to us what happened to Wayne. Ms. Jamison said she thought that was a great idea and if Mama needed her to keep us kids to catch a little break, by all means, please ask. Of course Mama said no, that she was fine and didn't need anything. I looked at Mama, and I could feel that she resented Ms. Jamison because we were hanging all over her. But she was comfort. She hugged us, she patted our backs, and she showed us love.

Feeling uncomfortable about what was happening before her very eyes with our affection for Ms. Jamison, Mama quickly told Ms. Jamison that she was getting us ready to return to school. Although Ms. Jamison was a mild-mannered lady, she wasn't easily dismissed this time. She told Mama she didn't mind hanging around to help out. She continued to tell her that Tommy was taking it so hard that she thought about getting him some counseling.

But Mama, with her quick lip and attitude, told Ms. Jamison, "You better tell that boy to get on his knees and pray and get over it. Wayne wasn't sick; he didn't have cancer or a bad heart. He took his own life. That boy was going to be worthless as a man if he couldn't cope cuz a few kids teased him about being in foster care. Hell, some of those kids have got rotten parents themselves, so he should have stood up to them."

At that point Ms. Jamison had heard enough. That day was the last time Ms. Jamison ever spoke to Mama. "Ms. Beatrice, I refuse to disrespect you, but what you are saying is just wrong. That young man was a beautiful boy with a loving soul. It's sad that there were only a few of us that saw it and the ones that he wanted to see it didn't, including you and his mother."

CHAPTER TWENTY-THREE

And before I could blink an eye, Ms. Jamison got up and told us kids she loved us and she would continue to pray for us. She also told Mama, "Ms. Beatrice, again it wasn't my intention to disrespect you, but I beg of you to stop bashing Wayne. He was a lovely young man." And she walked off the porch. I ran out of the door and hugged her. I wanted to tell her I understood what she said and ask would she please adopt me. However, she hugged me tightly and told me, "Neil, I love you."

After a few weeks, things started to get back to what we knew as normal. I was just beginning to deal with losing Wayne, and now something else would rock my inner core. Someone wanted to adopt Carole. My God, what else, I thought. I just buried my brother; now I had to lose Carole? Sure, Carole could be a handful, but I loved her. I found myself feeling devastated again.

Carole's impending adoption was quick. It hurt for a couple of reasons. I would no longer see my sister, and I wondered what it was about me that others deemed unworthy. Why didn't someone want me?

I will never forget the day Carole left. I remember Mama looking very sad. She didn't even look like that when she heard about Wayne's death. Carole, Eric, and I were playing outside. Mama stepped on the porch and asked Carole to come in.

She took a washcloth and wiped Carole's face, tightened up her hair bows, and walked her toward the door. I remember seeing the social worker, a man, and a woman standing in the front yard. And before I could say good-bye, Carole was walking out of the door with her new parents. That was the last time I saw Carole. I will never forget that pain. I often wonder if she ever thinks about me. Somehow I doubt it. I pray she is doing well in life. I'm sure if she still has that aggressive streak, she's probably a CEO right about now.

That night I prayed to God to help me deal with Carole suddenly leaving and, most importantly, Wayne's death. *God, please—please help me heal from everyone I love leaving me behind. Wayne was the only person in the world that loved me, and I miss him. I know my life will never be the same without Wayne. He showed me compassion and unconditional love. God, please let someone adopt me like they did Carole. I miss her.*

The only time I came close to being adopted was when Mama's son and daughter-in-law wanted to adopt Eric and me. But it never happened. However, they did send money and would come to visit two or three times a year to spend time with us.

I wondered how it would have been being adopted by the Johnsons. I thought about having a two-parent household and the fact that it was more believable that the Johnsons were our parents because they were much younger than Mama. No matter where we were, if people didn't know Mama, they would always say "your grandmother" to us. I was never embarrassed of Mama. But as far as the Johnsons adopting us, I would never find out what that was like, because both of them had health issues, so they thought it would be best if we stayed with Mama.

That night I lay in bed thinking about Ms. Jamison walking out of my life, because it was a done deal. Once you went against Mama, there was no turning back, so I knew Ms. Jamison would no longer be welcome. I had lost Carole and had the heartache of losing Wayne. I asked God, "What is it that I'm doing wrong? What can I do to please you, and why must this pain continue?"

CHAPTER TWENTY-FOUR

When I woke up, I looked at my body, and I didn't look the same. I was different. I was no longer the five-year-old little boy. I was thirteen. I finally understood my connection to God and his gift to me, so I wasn't surprised or scared. God heard me loud and clear, and I thanked him. I got on my knees and looked toward the sky and prayed, "God, you heard my heart, thank you. I will do my best to understand this gift that you have given me."

I prayed that with age Mama had become a more understanding person. I prayed that eight years had softened her heart and made her more loving. But that thought would soon change because I could hear her bellow to me that I didn't hang the clothes on the line the way she had showed me. I could never do enough to please her.

While Mama was yelling at me, Eric had a grin on his face. It was definitely apparent that Eric was truly her fair-haired son. He knew full well that Mama always had his back; it was eight years later, and nothing had changed. I walked toward her and handed her the clothes basket. She snatched the basket and walked outside toward the clothesline. I followed behind, hoping she would see that I wanted to learn. I sat down with no eye contact. She continued to rearrange the clothes to her satisfaction. So I decided to ask her. "Mama, what was wrong with the way I hung them up?"

"Neil, you need to pay attention to what I tell you. I told you that the clothespins should go one way. I don't ask you kids to do many chores that I can't do myself, but when I ask for help I need you to do it right."

"Yes, ma'am." I didn't say anything else. I sat there and watched her turn the clothespins the exact same way. To me, I hadn't done anything wrong, but I definitely didn't push the issue.

I looked around the neighborhood and noticed how much things had changed over the years, good and bad. Now drugs had become a part of our neighborhood. Cars would ride up to some of my older friends and neighbors, and with a quick exchange, I would see them being handed something and holding it tightly in their hands, pulling back pot or, in some cases, money. I could see Mama shaking her head, talking about how the neighborhood wasn't the same. Now I realized eight years had taken a toll on the neighborhood, and I didn't like it. But my goal was to keep my eyes on Mama, so I could learn the right way to hang clothes, because after all, all I wanted was her acceptance.

Years had passed since that fateful time in my life. But I thought about Wayne every day. I missed his love and his artwork; his talent was amazing. He would sketch for hours; now I understood that was his outlet. He was amazing, and I missed my brother.

CHAPTER TWENTY-FIVE

Being placed in foster care means you never understand your full worth. At least that was how I felt. I wondered all the time, what was it about me that was so awful that my biological parents didn't want to raise me? And being placed in foster care and treated unfairly, I found myself wondering, was there something I could have done to be better? Trying to escape my surroundings, I began to express myself with poetry and poems. It helped to release some of my feelings. But who was I kidding? Sometimes I was downright angry. Not only did I feel abandoned by my parents, but I felt abandoned by God. Although this journey was placed upon me, I felt it was unfair. I wanted a mother who appreciated the little gifts that I would bring her on Mother's Day. I wanted a father to teach me how to work on a car. I wanted a family.

On one particular day, I started to sketch and noticed a bird chirping loudly. I wondered for a split second if that bird had a mother. Yeah, it sounds stupid, but the smallest things made me take notice, because I didn't have parents. And nature could be cruel also. Birds were known to toss out their young if they didn't want them. I knew at thirteen that if I ever had children, they wouldn't want for anything. I promised God that I would be the best, most supportive father that I could be. I promised that I would never let my kids be without love.

I also decided that day that I wasn't going to be a statistic because of my situation. I didn't know what I wanted to do in life at this point, but whatever it was, I wanted to make a difference. I looked across the street, and I could see my other friends hanging out, some of them studying, playing cards, and, yep, still selling dope. One thing for sure I knew— that was not going to be in my future. That night I thought about how if Wayne was still alive, my life would have turned out so differently. Wayne would be an adult by now, and I'm sure with the love he had for me, I would be living with him and his biological brother. But the what-ifs had to stop; that wasn't my reality.

I walked onto the porch, and I could see something in Mama's face. I'd seen many looks from her over the years, but this one I hadn't seen before. She sat me down and told me to get washed up for dinner and to make sure I picked out something for school. Eric wasn't far behind. That night I said my prayers and asked God to keep me safe, and I told God I would do my best to be the man he made me to be. And for what-ever reason, that night I wondered about my father. Who was he, where was he, and, most of all, did he know about me?

CHAPTER TWENTY-SIX

The next morning I was still unsettled and I didn't know why, but I got ready for school. Eric and I headed out together. When I got to school everything was the same; in other words, everything was normal, as God had planned it. At thirteen, I was now in Ransom Middle School, and I was beginning to feel comfortable in my skin. I started making my own decisions, and I decided I was going to go out for football and basketball. I had found something that I was good at, and it was a stark contrast from just another day in foster care. I made decisions as a team player, and I enjoyed feeling and being accepted. I finally had a voice, and I made sure my opinion counted.

Joining the teams created a bond of brothers. I have to admit I was good at both basketball and football. Although things were getting better at school, the days proved to be harder at the Thompson household. The thought of things getting better the older I became proved to be devastatingly wrong. I loved Eric, but Mama continued to make such a difference between Eric and me that I started to resent him. It wasn't Eric's fault. But I did my best to continue playing sports as a diversion.

Mama never attended the games, and that made me sad, especially when my teammates' families came to cheer them on. Of course, Mama was getting up in age. She complained often that having kids in the household was beginning to take its toll on her. I kept praying that God would give me another blessing and remove me from the household. I knew I was too old for adoption, so I prayed I would wake up and be an adult. That would mean leaving Mama, Eric, and the rest far behind. And just when I thought things couldn't get worse in my life, something happened that would be forever etched in my heart.

I came home from school, and Mama was there waiting with a social worker I didn't know. Mama told me, "Neil, I packed a few things for you. You know I haven't been feeling well, so I'm going to send you to the Ninety-Nine Boys' Ranch in Gonzales in Florida for a while."

When she said that, I thought I would be going there for a few days to ride horses and mess around until she felt better. Not once did I think this would be permanent. I looked at her and nodded OK and prayed she would get better really soon. I told myself that at least I would have Eric at the ranch.

The social worker asked me if there was anything else I needed and told me that if there was, this would be the time to go get it. I walked toward the room I shared with Eric and noticed all of my things were packed. Not some of my things but all of them. There wasn't anything of mine left in the Thompson household that gave the impression that I had ever lived here. However, I brushed that off and continued to look around, looking for anything else I might need for a few days. I noticed that none of Eric's things had been touched. Eric's stuff was still intact. I walked out, and I noticed Mama just standing there, looking a little embarrassed. If you haven't realized it by now, there was nothing that embarrassed Mama. But I could see it in her face. Suddenly I realized I was the only one leaving today and that Eric was staying with Mama.

That day was the second time in my life that I became unwanted. I walked off the stoop and looked back. She looked at me, and that was the last time I would see her face for many, many years. In my heart, I didn't think I could feel less loved, but that familiar feeling was back again. I got into the car with the social worker and asked her, "Where are you taking me?"

She replied, "The boys' ranch." I don't know why I asked again; maybe I thought I didn't hear Mama correctly. But I had heard what she said the first time. I had often heard of the ranch from Mama when she would say, "You don't have to stay here, Neil; I can easily send you to Gonzales, and you know what that means." Little did I know that this would become a reality for me one day. I also heard about the ranch from the kids who would tease me. They would make comments like "Giddyap, horse, cuz you're gonna live on a ranch." But I never, ever thought that this would become my fate.

CHAPTER TWENTY-SEVEN

Riding out to the ranch was so surreal. It was about thirty minutes away, so for pretty much the whole ride, I rode in silence. I remember the social worker telling me, "Neil, everything will work out just fine for you; don't worry." But how could she tell me that? She had no idea what was in store for me. I had heard the horror stories, and I admit I found myself nervous. I didn't know what I could have done better with Mama. I had listened to her and obeyed her; I had done everything she asked of me. I couldn't understand what would make her send me away yet keep Eric.

I kept thinking my entire life has been centered around people not wanting me. Call it the gift or maybe the fact I knew that Mama preferred Eric over me, but I knew in my heart she was never coming for me. Arriving at the ranch, the nervousness I felt in my stomach was overwhelming. I could see older men and women moving around the halls. I saw some of the boys, and some of them were bigger than the adults. I tried to look tough because I didn't want anyone to know how scared I was. But this wasn't transitioning into a new foster home. If I'd been going to a new home, at least I would have had an idea of who I would be dealing with.

But this was a facility for so many unwanted boys, most importantly troubled boys. I wasn't troubled, but I was definitely unwanted. I looked around and was introduced to my counselor. I sat down, and for the first time in a very long time, I realized I was truly on my own. I didn't have

Mama, Eric, my other foster brothers and sisters, the babies, or even the neighbors that I had grown up with over the many years of living with Mama.

That day at the ranch I built up a defense that would carry me through my entire life. Growing up the way I did, it was hard for me to understand why people cried and became so distraught when family members passed or when people moved away. The emotion of caring wasn't taught. It should come naturally, but growing up in foster care and living in a boys' home meant it wasn't natural for me. I never had time to digest real love. Foster care for me was an empty and lonely existence. I had done my best to fit into the Thompson household, but Mama had at times made me feel unwanted. I had done my best to ignore that hurt, but no matter how much I tried, it hurt, so I built up a defense. Being placed at the ranch was life changing to say the least.

I was surrounded by boys who weren't just unwanted but troubled. Some of them were in for robbery, some were drug dealers, and some of them had mental issues—it was a vast mixture of boys. I was also surrounded by boys who had parents, good parents in some cases, but for whatever reason, they had acted out and were placed at the ranch. I used to look at them and want to scream at the top of my lungs, "You stupid assholes, I would do anything to have parents or a parent who wanted me!"

But what hurt the most was that I had thought I had a family. I had thought Mama would always be there. No matter how many times she had threatened to send me away, in my heart I never thought she would. Then with no indication or reason, I was simply told my time was up.

With Mama's decision, I realized I could be thrown away like an old pair of shoes. God, that hurt. Being placed at the ranch was my new beginning, and I could either fight it or go with it. Having no other choice, I decided to accept my new situation and fight this fight. So I did what I do best, and I adapted. I never felt sorry for myself or the hand that was dealt me. Yeah, I questioned it, but I was a fighter. I had to look at this as positively as possible. Because if I fought against things I couldn't change, it would only stifle my progress. While at the ranch, I followed the rules and, for the most part, met some really good friends. Of course there were times that I had to knuckle up to prove I was no pushover. But most of all I accepted what was handed to me and pressed on.

Surprisingly, the counselors and staff were pretty caring. They did their best to treat all the boys with respect. They made a tough situation as pleasant as possible. We were reprimanded when needed, but it wasn't like those horror stories I had heard about. We were treated with dignity and respect. So being placed at the ranch turned out to be a comfortable existence for me. Who knew?

The whole time I was there, Mama never came to visit. In fact, it was years before I saw Mama or Eric again. It's funny; I thought going to the ranch would be devastating, but it helped shape me. One thing was for sure: I didn't have to remain with Mama and let her continued favoritism of Eric sink deeper and deeper into my heart. I continued playing sports, and that helped fill a void. Holidays were made special. Gifts were donated at Christmas, and the staff also brought us gifts. One day, Mr. Boyd, one of the counselors, came in and mentioned that I resembled a family he knew in the area. I was excited yet hesitant to think that I might have biological family still in the area.

He asked me if I would be interested in digging into my past if he contacted them. He said the resemblance was uncanny. Of course I was excited, thinking that this could be true and that I could have an actual connection to blood relatives.

And before I knew it, Mr. Boyd took me to see my family. I was introduced to my aunt Anita, my uncle Ronnie, and, to my delight, a sister. Life could change so dramatically. In the blink of an eye, your whole world could be turned around. My sister was in the military, and that was so impressive to me. Although it was nice finally having a family, it was still an adjustment. Aunt Anita and Uncle Ronnie didn't get legal custody of me; however, they became my guardians, so I could finally leave the ranch.

My entire senior year, I stayed with Aunt Anita and Uncle Ronnie. I was grateful, but there were times that I felt I was also being taken advantage of. I was no longer a teenager; I was a man. I had pretty much raised myself with the help of outsiders. So maybe part of the problem was that I was too independent. Maybe things would have been different had I met them earlier, and maybe I could have been molded to fit in better. Both my aunt and uncle made me feel like a chauffeur, landscaper, and all around handyman. Don't misunderstand me; I was thankful for them, but I paid my dues, I worked and gave them money to stay with them because I was appreciative, but there comes a time in your life when you know you are being taken advantage of. After all, I was no longer a kid. But you turned the other cheek and looked at the positive.

Nevertheless, I had a family, and I did my best to fit in—the story of my life. I continued going to high school and working. I was still in the cadet program. The program had given me structure over the years. I had started the program while in Ransom Middle School. And now that I would be graduating soon, I knew I wanted to continue my life with this type of structure. And having a sister in the military just solidified that desire.

I must say, one of the best days of my life was the day I graduated from high school. All I kept thinking was I now had true independence. A lot had happened over these uncertain years and the challenges I had faced. But believe it or not, I knew I would come full circle in a good way. Damn, it wasn't easy, I have to admit. The day I graduated, I remember looking into the audience and having a flashback like so many others over the years. I wondered if my mother realized that this should be the year that I graduated. I'm sure she didn't; it was wishful thinking on my part.

I hated feeling these emotions; feeling vulnerable made me feel weak. I graduated from Pensacola High School, and it was time to put this chapter of my life far behind. After all the prayers, dreams, visions, and wanting to take control over my life, it was a reality today. I was now in control, and I was not about to fail.

CHAPTER TWENTY-EIGHT

Finally the day had arrived when I could make my own decisions. No longer did my biological mother, my foster mother, the Ninety-Nine Boys' Ranch, or the state have any say in Neil Washington's life. Soon after graduating, I moved out of Uncle Ronnie and Aunt Anita's home. I continued working at Water Burger and going to community college. I wanted to do something bigger with my life, and I wasn't going to let my circumstances define me. Although I encountered roadblocks and obstacles, I wasn't going to be another troubled African American male. I didn't know what I wanted to do thus far, but whatever it was, I wanted to be damn good at it. Graduating was such a milestone for me. I could finally look at the world in a whole different light.

I was still on the fence as to exactly what I wanted to do. I didn't want to waste time, so I pursued a few things. Having the cadet program behind me helped me to make sound decisions. I looked into the Pensacola police program, but I also started thinking more about the military. The reality of working and going to college wasn't easy. Supporting myself and maintaining an education had its challenges at times. Although I was still focusing on my education, after a couple of years I decided it was time to go in a different direction.

So I enlisted in the United States Army. I enjoyed working as a police cadet, but I wanted to explore other avenues and get out of Pensacola. Don't get me wrong, I loved home, but it was time I explored what else God had in store for me. Somehow I knew staying here wasn't it. Ironically, I was notified by the First Judicial Circuit Court of Florida on February 13, 1987, that I had passed all the necessary tests to qualify as a police officer, level one. In fact, my score was 83.54. I was so proud of myself. Yet again I didn't have anyone to share such great news and my accomplishments with. Although you would think after so many years of being on my own, I would have been used to not having someone to share great news or any news with. And although I felt tough because I had to be, I never got used to having to keep everything of importance to myself.

Sure, my friends and associates were proud and happy for me. But having family to celebrate with…I've never had that true feeling. After connecting with my sister, it was nice having her support, and that made me feel good. Vivian was always supportive. So I guess you could say things were turning around for me.

But nothing could compare to having a mother or father say, "Good job, Neil. I'm proud of you, son." I have never heard those words. Nevertheless, I continued to reach for the stars. I was headed to Fort Dix, New Jersey, for basic training. I arrived at Fort Dix, and I was so excited. I knew from the first day of basic training that the military was my saving grace. I loved everything about it. The structure and, once again, the bond it gave me were wonderful.

I remember a letter going out informing family members that we had arrived safely. It started with "Greetings, your son has arrived safely at the Reception Battalion at Fort Dix and has embarked on the challenging transition from civilian to soldier." I remember looking at that and thinking I wasn't someone's son, so they could have saved the paper and the time spent sending it.

And then there would be the final letter informing and inviting family members to attend graduation. "You are cordially invited to attend the Basic Training Graduation at Doughboy Field, May 8, 1987, at nine o'clock in the morning. This ceremony marks the end of the eight weeks of Basic Training. We hope that you will be able to attend." I knew no one would attend, because, after all, the letter went to Mama's house, so once again this would be another journey that I would have to travel alone.

Suddenly I felt all of those emotions of being on my own and that empty feeling that had been with me my entire life. I would look into the stands, and no one would be there. Well, no one for me, that is. Nevertheless, I graduated from basic training, and I was damn proud of myself. I was so excited that I had accomplished this decision of joining the army; now it was really time to start my life. Although no one came to graduation, I was determined to enjoy my day to the fullest.

I was invited by so many soldiers who had become my friends to share their day with them and their families. Although their invitations were kind, I didn't want to be a third wheel, so I eventually went back to my barracks. I watched other friends and soldiers get hugs, kisses, and love from their family members. Fathers, mothers, sisters, brothers, and extended family members gave accolades to their young soldiers. But that day I was determined not to let this deter me from enjoying my day; nevertheless, it still hurt, and I felt empty. Yes, I should have been used to this, but sometimes I wondered if I would ever get used to it.

Time can become your worst enemy or your best friend. So having nothing but time on my hands, I began the process of figuring out what I wanted the army to do for my life. And that night I decided I was going to continue to press on and become the best soldier I could be. Sure, it was early in the decision process, but being a soldier just felt right. Once again, this was another turning point in my life.

In the military, I did my best not to talk down to my soldiers. Of course, there were times I had to put a foot in their asses, and there were times I found myself thinking I should have taken a different approach. When I fell short, I tried to recognize my shortcomings. I would literally say to myself, "Neil, you could have handled that better," because I knew that feeling oh so well. I knew how being talked to poorly was always like a punch in the gut; it stripped so much of my self-esteem away. I always did my best to listen and help my soldiers when I could. I thanked God for what I experienced in foster care. It had taught me the valuable lesson of listening to my soldiers, even when their excuses were often just that—excuses. I never let my rank intimidate anyone. I wanted them to understand that I was there to listen and learn.

CHAPTER TWENTY-NINE

I loved the military, and I can honestly say I enjoyed my job to the fullest. The military allowed me to leave Pensacola and fulfill other dreams. I was stationed abroad several times over the years, but the greatest gift of all was when I got stationed at Aberdeen Proving Ground in Maryland. Little did I know that such a little state was going to offer me a lifetime of love and everlasting memories. One night I decided to go to the local Veterans of Foreign Wars post, and to my delight, I saw this petite, beautiful woman who would eventually become my wife. Finally I discovered the piece to my puzzle that had been missing my entire life: I found the love of my life. I met my wife, and I never looked back. I looked forward to becoming a great husband and soldier. It was challenging at times, because my career would take precedence sometimes. But that's why it was important to me to have a woman who would hold me down. I'm sure it was difficult at times for my wife, relocating and just being married to a soldier, but she never complained. She was the backbone, and I couldn't have asked for a better companion.

It isn't easy being married to a soldier. I needed someone strong to maintain the household without missing a beat. And I thanked God for her every day. I listened to horror stories of other soldiers about their wives or husbands not paying bills or not being the best parents, and it made me appreciate my wife even more. My wife was sent from God, and I adored the woman she was; she was beautiful inside and out. She raised our daughter with a firm but loving hand, but she was the love of my life, and I wouldn't know how to live without her. I was blessed!

Meeting my wife gave me an appreciation for family. She had a very close family unit. I loved my new extended family; instead of celebrating important holidays or milestones alone, I could finally have Christmas dinners, Thanksgivings, and birthday parties as a family unit. But there were times when I continued to feel lonely, because no matter how I looked at it, or how much I loved my wife's family, they were still family simply by marriage. I admired them because they had such a strong bond, and they welcomed and loved me, but the desire to have my own family was always on the surface.

As my career progressed, I found so much about the army that I loved. I loved mentoring young soldiers of all backgrounds. I admit I was driven a little harder to mentor soldiers who didn't come from the best backgrounds and, most importantly, the soldiers who grew up surrounded by heartache. But all of my soldiers were special to me because I was supposed to take care of them. I took that oath in the military to heart, and I did my best to stay true to it.

I was fair to all my soldiers, but for the soldiers who had troubled backgrounds I tried to instill in them that their backgrounds didn't define who they were. Circumstances didn't define me; they built the man I became, and that was what God intended. I was passionate about letting people know who I really was. I wasn't ashamed of being a foster kid, because it didn't define me. I would sit soldiers down and express to them that no matter who they were they could overcome, especially if they had the career path of the military behind them.

It shocked so many of them when I opened up about my childhood. They made comments like, "Get out of here, First Sergeant. You look like you had it all." Other soldiers would say, "Then how did you become a first sergeant with your background?" But if there was anything that made me proud, it was when soldiers told me, "Thanks for believing in me." Man, that was a feeling that made my military career all worth it. I wouldn't have traded my military career for anything. It opened up many doors and put closure to so many others.

CHAPTER THIRTY

Wow, twenty years, where did the time go? I thought. With the uncertainty of the military, my wife and I started talking about me retiring. I was satisfied with my military career and started reflecting on what it was that I hadn't accomplished that would solidify my retirement. And it hit me: I wanted to go airborne. Although I waited much further in my career than most soldiers, it was still nagging at me to do it. And, hell yeah, I had the naysayers and those who thought I was too old, but nevertheless, I was always up for the challenge. Hell, I was used to the naysayers after growing up in foster care. I wanted to pursue my last military goal. If my background taught me anything, it taught me that nothing was impossible. And after my wife supported my decision, I could have cared less what anyone else thought. I left in the summer, and I was excited. I met young soldiers and realized I was old enough to be their fathers.

I wasn't a conceited person, but I felt confident that I could keep up with the rigorous training. And, damn, was it rigorous. I kept up with those young soldiers, but it wasn't easy. I was now their peer and not "First Sergeant." As time drew closer to my actual jump, I was nervous, excited, anxious—all the emotions wrapped in one. I can't say that I was scared, but now the what-ifs were beginning to pop in my head. The night before my jump, I prayed that God would continue to look over me. This could truly be a life-or-death situation. And I had a family to think about. But I felt confident and, most of all, in control.

Finally the day arrived. I remember thinking about my wife and kids, and suddenly everything was put into perspective—talk about surreal. I stood there waiting to jump, and a million thoughts ran through my mind. But our instructors continued to encourage us and instill in us that we shouldn't focus on anything other than the importance of this jump. The fact that I was nervous as hell and the thought that I was finally about to fulfill my last military dream was overwhelming. I heard the instructor counting down, and before I could think about it, I jumped. Free falling was so amazing. It was so peaceful. I felt a feeling I'd never felt before; it's hard to explain, but it was a peace that I'd never experienced. Falling closer to the ground was exhilarating. It seemed as if I was in the air forever. I closed my eyes for a split second, and I saw Wayne.

My God! My God! It was Wayne, and before I could say anything, I felt the most excruciating pain of my life. I fell safely, but I landed horribly. I lay there in pain as the other instructors and medical staff arrived. I couldn't explain it, but this was the worst pain I could have imagined. My God, I thought, what have I done? Lying there, I knew I had broken something, and given the fact my ankle seemed to be exploding, that was my guess. My whole body was in pain. I was in so much pain that I had an out-of-body experience because of this excruciating, unbearable feeling.

The phrase "my God, what have I done?" kept playing in my head. I heard voices, but I couldn't concentrate on anything. As I was rushed to the hospital, all I could think about was my family. I didn't know whether to let my wife know, but of course I had to. The realization of not completing something I set out to do was now a reality. And call it what you want, but I was pissed and disappointed that I didn't succeed. Foster care made me want to do better at everything no matter how big or small it was because the odds were so highly stacked against me. Sometimes I didn't realize it, but I always wanted to be the best at everything I did. Not completing this jump was just as painful to me as the pain in my body. I was my own worst critic. I've been that way all of my life. I expected perfection.

When I arrived at the hospital, the doctor told me that I had broken my ankle. The surgeon and the military instructors assured me that I had completed the jump successfully but simply landed wrong. Well, all I could hear from that was that I hadn't completed the mission. Nevertheless, I still had my life, so I had to put the mishap in perspective. God spared my life, and I was thankful! It could have definitely ended much worse, including ending in death. After that realization hit me, for the first time I thought, what the hell was I thinking, jumping out of a damn plane?

Suddenly I felt an overwhelming sense of peace. I didn't know if it was the painkillers or what, but I was feeling pretty damn peaceful. I lay there, and the surgeon said he would be performing surgery immediately. Whatever the hell I was given for pain was damn good; I suddenly didn't feel my busted ankle. I looked up, and there was Wayne again. I started to cry because there was my brother whom I had missed over the years. He was still the young boy I remembered; he looked the same. I was comforted that he was here with me because I didn't have my wife and kids. I had no other family members I could have called other than Vivian and Eric, and I didn't call them either.

I couldn't believe Wayne was here. How could he be? He had died many, many years ago. The first question I asked him was why did he leave me, and I told him that I had missed him over the years. He held my hand and said softly, "Little brother, I've been with you this whole time. I never left you. I told you I would never leave you, and I never did." But in my heart I kept thinking, how could he say he didn't leave me? He did when he killed himself. I lay there confused and dazed, but I wanted some answers.

I heard a soft voice, and it was God. *"My son, Wayne was never in the flesh. He was sent by me to watch over you."* I could see Wayne standing there, plain as day, not saying a word.

Wayne grabbed my hand and stroked it gently. *"Neil,"* he said softly. *"I've never been in the flesh, baby brother.* As I struggled to understand, he continued to speak.

I was sent by God when you were at Escambia Hospital. No one could see me but you. I was sent to give you strength, encouragement, comfort, and, most of all, love. I was here all along to protect you. Neil, remember 'incoming, incoming, First Sergeant' and a loud explosion—and then silence, and you felt an overwhelming sense of peace? Neil, only God can determine how we go off this earth. And although that happened, God decided against it. He wanted you to continue this journey because, baby brother, you have so much ahead of you. You have a bigger fight to fight; just remember that. There were so many ways you could have ended up. For instance, I was also to instill in you that taking your life was never the way; I know that was one of the worst days of your life. So when you went to the boys' ranch, do you know how many friends you helped? Sometimes you would talk about suicide and give them strength not to take that avenue. You would have never known to do that if not for me. But that day strengthened you in so many ways that shaped you into the man you are today. You became a man that day.

That lesson taught you to stay focused and pursue your dreams. Look how far you've come, baby brother. Your love for me made you dedicate your heart and soul to being the best man you could be. And, my God, you have. God sends angels to special people, and you were special from the day you were given life. Now God is sending you to instill in so many people that same goodness of life. Do you know how many people you have blessed through your story?

Do you know how many people respect you because the odds were stacked against you? You have told your story, and believe me when I tell you, you've given strength to more people than you know. That was your duty from God. God makes no mistakes, Neil. Continue to tell your story. You will continue this mission, and you will see. You will reach people you never thought you could. You will encourage the masses; I don't know how yet, because God only tells me what I'm supposed to know, but you will reach many people with your message. Do whatever God has for you to do; don't fight it. It's your obligation.

I have always been here, Neil, but only you saw me because that's what God wanted. Eric wasn't sad for me because he never knew me; neither did Mama. Think about it, Neil, have you ever thought about me since you were little?

I couldn't understand why I had never thought about Wayne while growing up. It was as if I had totally forgotten about him. I guess I had. So I asked him, why would God give him to me and then let him be forgotten, and once again he asked me, "So you never thought about me at all?"

I smiled because I hadn't. Wayne smiled and said, "*My gift was to you only. Sometimes God is an all-about-me God, and I was for you alone.*"

Wayne smiled and spoke again.

I told you I would see you again, baby brother, and I never break my promises because I answer to God. But now you've become a wonderful man, husband, and father, and you have blessed so many people in your life you will never know. My job is done; you've made me proud, but most of all, you've made God proud. You will make out just fine in surgery. My last gift to you is this: you will heal, and no one, including your doctors, will understand it. You will be walking on your own in no time. But the

99

power of God is this: you will return home to base at the proving ground and go back to leading PT like you've never broken your ankle. People won't believe how you are able to lead PT, because it will be a miracle. You will see. Continue to be a blessing, baby brother, but you're all grown up. My job here is done.

He leaned down, hugged me, and whispered in my ear that he loved me. And he was gone. Damn, I thought, these are some powerful-ass drugs. The next morning I woke up and saw a sketched picture next to my bed with "*I love you, baby brother, Wayne.*" I smiled but thought they must have gotten the wrong patient, because I didn't know a Wayne.

CHAPTER THIRTY-ONE

Call it a miracle, but I healed in no time. But before I could wrap my head around healing so quickly, I received orders to go to Korea. And once again I had to transition. However, while in Korea I realized I was tired of leaving my family. After Korea I was supposed to report straight to Fort Stewart, Georgia, and then to Iraq. So the decision was made: my wife and I decided it was time to retire. I thought about it, and although the decision was hard, I realized it was time to start a new journey in my life. I had served my country for twenty years and I had no regrets. I wanted to spend time with my family, and who are we kidding—I didn't know if I would come back from Iraq.

But damn, twenty years seemed to have flown by. I retired and, with the help of a family member, was blessed to get a great job. I didn't pursue working on base; I wanted something totally different. It was time to be a full-time husband and father. Although my children were independent, it felt good being home with the family. I began civilian life with appreciation and a desire to start living life.

But nothing could have prepared me for what was about to happen. Oh my God, the call that I had anticipated my whole life finally came. My sister called to tell me it was time to come to Florida and finally meet our mother in the flesh. I was so nervous; I really didn't know how to feel. The very next day I got on a flight; after all, time was of the essence. I started thinking about the outcome and finally having the opportunity to stand face-to-face with my mother.

After being in the army for twenty years, you would think I would be used to flying, but I hated it. I always tried to find things to distract me when I flew. So instead of concentrating on my dislike of flying, I planned to listen to my iPod. But without fail I started thinking, and before I could stop myself, once again my past started to flood my mind.

The year 1984 had so much significance in my life. After graduating in 1984, I also started searching for my mother. I finally had an address, so I wrote her a letter. I kept thinking that the fact that I had graduated from high school would help her understand that I didn't want anything, just the opportunity to meet her.

Knowing she knew who Aunt Anita and Uncle Ronnie were, I expressed to her that I was no longer living with them and that I was independent. I explained some of what had happened while living with my aunt and uncle. I made it clear that I loved them both and appreciated them for taking me in. But I felt as if they felt I should be forever indebted to them. I told her that Uncle Ronnie wanted me to drive him around and be at his beck and call.

I didn't want her to think I was ungrateful, so I tried to express it with a little more clarity. I wrote that in my senior year I had a job, but I always felt that my uncle and aunt expected me to not just lend a hand but that their hands were always out. Trust me; I carried my weight and then some. Believe me; I was appreciative, but I also wanted to be appreciated. I felt that by expressing this to her and explaining that I was on my own and doing just fine, somehow she would respect the young man I had become without her.

In hindsight, maybe I thought that if she was aware of my difficult situation with my aunt and uncle, then maybe, just maybe, she would soften her heart and be eager to meet me. But nothing on this earth could have prepared me for what I received back. The hatred this woman had for me was unfathomable. She returned her response on the same envelope that I had mailed to her. In other words, she tore the envelope open and returned her response. Her hatred for me was so great that I didn't even rate having her respond on a piece of paper.

Her response spoke volumes, and her hatred toward me was unexplainable. And what you will read below is quoted from her response and is just a part of the hurtful words she sent to me.

> *I have two daughters and a son. You and I have been disowned since birth, and whoever you are, you aren't better than me. I have no remembrance of you, nor do I want to. I was told by a judge it was over when I signed papers. I hate you. You've got some nerve bothering me. Your picture and letters I tore up. I'll put you in jail for harassing me. We are moving out of town. Love whoever it is that raised you. I'm not your mother, understand? Whoever fed or clothed you, that's your parent, not me. Nor will I ever be. I will never own you. You've been looking at too many movies or reading too many novels. I don't even know who you are. Don't you dare call me mom.*

I sat there that day with hurt in my heart that I tried to ignore, but imagine the woman who had carried you for nine months saying such hurtful things and claiming she didn't know you.

I was not only hurt but dumbfounded. I could lie and say I was tough and that I was OK with the outcome. But nothing would have or could have prepared me for that letter. This lady truly hated me, and I didn't know why. I was no longer the little boy she gave away to the Pensacola foster care system. I was a grown man reaching out to get to know this woman, not with a motive, needing money, or wanting anything but some answers. I wanted to ask her what it was about the bright-eyed little boy she had carried for nine months—what it was about me—that caused her to give me away to the state when she had kept all of her other children. I was anxious, wanting to ask all the questions that I had thought about over the years.

However, the first time I laid eyes on my mother was in the morgue. Yes, my mother had passed away. Vivian and I walked slowly down the hall, and over twenty-seven years later, I finally saw my mother. Although I had never seen her in the flesh during those twenty-seven years, I had reached out to her after I found a good address for her and wrote her. Her hateful, derogatory response when she returned my letter expressed that she hated me, had given me up, and didn't have any desire to ever meet me. She had kids, and I wasn't one of them. Well, if I was a cruel person I guess you could say I got the last laugh, but all I felt was hurt and pain. Nevertheless, I finally got to meet her. She couldn't hug me or see how much of a man I had become or how excited I was to finally meet her. But most importantly, I would never get the opportunity to ask her all the questions I wanted to ask. I looked down to see this well-kept older woman. In all honesty, she looked very familiar to me.

It was strange; I didn't feel much of anything, yet I still felt compassion. I stroked her hand and tried to grasp why this woman hadn't wanted to raise me, let alone get to know me as an adult. Reflecting on the things she had said in her letter, most people would have hated her, but looking down on her, I realized she was a sad, pathetic, unhappy, bitter woman. Realistically speaking, you can't hate someone you don't know. She didn't hate me; she hated herself.

And before I could collect my thoughts or digest everything, the funeral director asked Vivian and me who would be paying for the funeral. In that moment I looked at my sister, and we decided to split the difference. That was the first time I realized or heard that my mother didn't have enough insurance money to be laid to rest, and I didn't think twice about contributing money to a perfect stranger.

It's funny how life has a way of throwing curve balls. Imagine, the same lady who hated me needed me in the end. The children she raised couldn't bury her. It was kind of ironic, pathetic, and poignant. She hated me and had no desire whatsoever to get to know me. But in the end, I still had the last say. God is funny, isn't he? He makes you bow when you least expect it. I wasn't bitter; I felt sorry for this woman. If she had gotten to know me, maybe her life would have turned out better. I can guarantee you this—she wouldn't have needed a perfect stranger to pay for her going-home service.

Although she didn't want to raise me, if she had allowed me to get to know her twenty-seven years before, I would have cared for her in her sickness and old age. She would have been able to depend on me, her son. Whether she needed a little spending money, a word of inspiration, someone to call and say "How are you feeling, Mom," —or even "Ms. Gale"—a few dollars to play bingo or attend a church function with, or a "Happy Mother's Day" card with a little money in it, I would have helped her, but most importantly, she would not have lain on a cold slab in the morgue with uncertainty about how she would be laid to rest.

But I wasn't her son. I was a stranger on the street who had to bury this woman whom I didn't get to know and, most importantly, who didn't want to get to know me. So when you think you will never need someone, don't speak or think too fast, because you never know what God has in store. Sometimes people think their paths won't ever cross, but before you decided to write someone off because you don't like them, need them, or think they're unworthy of getting to know you, remember that you never know what today is, because today could just be the day that your paths may cross. I can guarantee you that my mother never thought she would ever see me again, because she had chosen to disregard me. Little did she know that the one she hated would be the one she needed in the end. God has the last say; never underestimate fate.

CHAPTER THIRTY-TWO

On the flight back to Maryland, I realized something: closure never came to me. Yes, I finally saw the face of my mother. But I would never feel her embrace. The only affection I got from her was a touch of her cold hand. My children would never get the opportunity to see their grandmother. As hard as I thought I was, I wanted the happy ending, the closure that I saw in the movies. I envied Antwone Fisher, who met his mom, but most of all he connected with wonderful, loving members of his family. But this wasn't my ending. The more I thought about it, the angrier I became, so instead of rehashing this disappointment, I decided that after the flight attendant came around with some liquor, which I needed desperately, I would take a nap. However, walking out of the funeral home that day, I had picked up a Bible that was lying on the table in the lobby. Once again dreading this flight, I figured I would read the Bible before I let a gin and Pepsi get to my head and take my nap.

I fell asleep, and suddenly everything that was once blurred and confusing to me as a little boy came full circle. Now the faces that said thank you so many years ago were a reality. Those men and women I'd seen as a child were the young soldiers I had helped over my military career. The gentleman was Mr. Boyd from the Ninety-Nine Boys' Ranch who had helped me locate my biological family. The beautiful petite woman was my wife, and the little girl with the sandals, who smiled and hugged me, was my daughter, Ciara. My God, the little boy thanking me for fighting for him and not letting him become a statistic was my son, Christopher.

I had Christopher before I got married, and although I loved him very much, he remained with his mother in another state. But I would have never left my son, and I made attempts to make sure he knew he was loved and that he always had a father in me. My wife loved and adored Christopher as if he was her own. At one point I thought I would be stationed in the area, but once Christopher came to live with us and was getting settled in our family unit, the army told me otherwise. So my wife not only raised our daughter but our son as well. Having to leave my wife and two kids was just part of the job.

Years later, my son joined the army reserves; now it made sense that he was the young man thanking me with his uniform on. I am proud of my son. I guess it was in his blood, and my handsome son is now married to a lovely young lady. My daughter is beautiful and a talented and up-and-coming singer. They are both amazing individuals in their own right. I am proud of both of my children; they are focused and they are both go-getters. Pursuing their dreams and always challenging themselves to be the best at whatever they put their minds to. They both reach for the impossible, and I must say, they are well-rounded young adults, and I am proud to be their father.

The older gentleman who had told me that I made him look like he did when he was young and was happy that I was home safe was Mr. King from a family barbershop. My wife's aunt owned a hair salon and barbershop, so when I retired, she welcomed me with open arms to barber for a few months while getting acclimated to civilian life.

But what was the most surprising acknowledgment from my childhood vision was the older lady who had thanked me for everything I had done and expressed to me that, "You turned out to be a wonderful young man, and thanks for all your help. You've been a true blessing to me." The woman was my mother; I remembered this was the same well-kept lady from the funeral home, and that was why she looked so familiar. I was taken aback, yet I felt excited. In all honesty, I didn't know how to feel. It was plain as day; this was the same woman whose hand I had stroked in the funeral parlor. As I reflected on this, the woman spoke to me again.

Neil, understand something. God is the Almighty; he knew what quality of life you would have had with me, and you would not have turned out to be the wonderful man, husband, and father you are today. I couldn't have given you the foundation that you deserved. I had much deeper issues with myself. I was not saying that my other children were more special than you were by keeping them. But this was much deeper than I could ever express. God had far bigger plans for you. You turned out to be a wonderful young man, and thanks for all your help. You've been a true blessing to me. I'm ashamed that I didn't let you into my life. You were unwanted in life, I'm ashamed to say, but you were embraced in death. Forgive me, son.

There was that word I had longed to hear from my mother, "son." I didn't know how to feel; I didn't know if this was real or not. But what I decided that day was that if it felt so right, it must have been real, and call me crazy, but if that was what closure felt like, then it was good enough for me. My heart no longer felt hardened or, for that matter, heavy. I felt at ease, but most of all, I felt some peace. But God still had one last thing for me.

I heard the pilot announce that we would be landing at Baltimore-Washington International Airport and to prepare for a smooth landing. I looked down at the Bible that was lying on my lap, and it was open to the scripture Romans 14:11, "For it is written: 'As I live,' saith the Lord, 'every knee shall bow to me, and every tongue shall confess to God.'" I smiled and thanked God; my mother had done just that.

CHAPTER THIRTY-THREE

The journey had finally come to an end when I realized my mother didn't hate me. She wasn't happy with herself. Later I found out that the man she truly loved had shipped out and left her behind. I realized that if my mother had kept me, she would have had a constant reminder of the man she had loved and lost when she looked into my eyes. It was sad that someone could take such a heartfelt, loving situation like giving birth and turn it into despair. I wondered how many women had given their children up because someone broke their heart. Although I wished my mother could have loved herself, and especially me, more, I was glad she hadn't had an abortion, killed me once I was born, or kept me and mistreated me. So all in all, she did the best thing she could have done.

My father was in the navy. Maybe the military was in my DNA. I had also reached out to my father in 1986. I wrote a letter expressing to him that I had no ill feelings about what happened back in 1965, because the greatest gift he had given me was the gift of life. I didn't have a concrete address; furthermore, I wasn't trying to destroy this man by popping out of the blue. If he was still alive, I figured he would be married, and I definitely didn't want to interfere in his life with such news.

There were procedures in place, so I had to contact the Department of Veterans Affairs. Following the process, the Department of Veterans Affairs couldn't locate him either. They needed more information. And

I didn't have much to go on myself. I never found my father, and maybe that was best. God has done well by me so far, so I'm not complaining.

———

In a perfect world, all children would be born to parents who adore them. But we don't live in a perfect world. It doesn't matter what color you are, what your sexual preference is, or how much money you make. If you want a child and you can give that child unconditional, healthy love, why should it matter? See, this was my life; I didn't read about it—I lived it. I grew up as a statistic.

There is paper work in Pensacola, Florida, at Escambia Hospital from February 11, 1966, saying "Baby Boy Washington." But I am not Baby Boy Washington anymore. My names are Mr. Washington, Dad, Husband, First Sergeant Washington, and, most of all, Neil Washington, a man who loves to be alive. I am not a statistic; I am a survivor, and I am damn proud of the man I have become.

You see, when the odds are stacked against you, circumstance can be stacked like a mountain in front of you to see how you deal with it. You can sit there and look at the mountain, move it, or go around it. Don't let anyone determine how great you can be. Society, family, friends, and circumstances do not determine the person you are. God has the last call, and call me crazy, but my circumstance wasn't going to define me. So if you aren't sure who you are, look toward the heavens and let the one and only one determine that. I promise you this: the little boy who once had no name became the man that I am today. You see, I'm not perfect, and I'm not a rich man by any means, but what I do know is if God is guiding your steps, you can't fall, so keep reaching for the stars, and let God do the rest. Neil Washington did. Foster care can be cruel to so many, but it can also shape a person. Foster care can be a wonderful life; it can be loving and nurturing.

There are wonderful foster parents who adore the children placed in their homes. Although I had some regrets with my foster mother, she taught me some very valuable lessons, and I know she loved me. I often think that if my foster mother had not been so strict, who's to say what kind of man I would be today? She taught me so much as a little boy, and those lessons have stayed with me as an adult. In 1995, Mama Thompson passed away. It's funny; when I visited her, she never knew who I was, but when I put on my military uniform, she beamed and always smiled and was elated. I remember looking at Mama in her casket and thinking how far I had come from that little boy. I felt that when she saw me in my uniform she knew she had laid down the foundation for me to be a better man. You may think I have regrets with Mama, but I don't; I have no regrets whatsoever.

I am thankful that things have continued to move forward with other ethnicities and other avenues for people to adopt, because at the end of the day, who doesn't want to be loved?

Thank God things have changed in the twenty-first century; now, interracial adoption is the norm. In other words, we've come a long way. Thank God for people wanting children who may not fit the typical mold of mirroring them.

After growing up in foster care, I challenge people who say how dare a white couple, or other couples of different ethnicities, try to adopt a foster child who doesn't resemble them? Try telling that to a little girl or boy just praying for someone to love them enough to get them out of the foster care system. Some people question gay parents wanting to adopt and love an innocent child, but I would have loved to have been with any supportive, nurturing, and, most importantly, loving family. Until this day, I still question the ignorance of people who have no idea how children feel growing up in foster care; they have many opinions, yet they don't try to adopt. They have the nerve to question someone else who cares enough to take in a child who may otherwise never get a home or love. I would have appreciated and adored a family of any color wanting me. You have those who say, "How can you learn about your heritage if you are adopted by someone from another race?" My question in response is, "Where are you when the foster children are waiting with their bags packed?" Just what I thought—nowhere to be found.

At the end of the day, how many children knew their history with their biological parents? I mean, you really can't speak for children like me; you just can't. Somehow knowing that my great-great-grandfather was the only black man who owned two pigs, five chickens, and an out-house in "Maga-Slap-Me," Mississippi, would not have mattered much to me. Growing up in the system for so many years, do you really think I would have turned down a good, stable home, with parents who wanted me permanently? Let's be real. The historical significance of one's ancestors to a foster child is just unimportant. For the parents who didn't mirror me or have the same sexual preference as me, I would have loved to have had the opportunity to be placed in a family like theirs—just because they wanted me.

Love does conquer many things. Love conquers mirror images or sexual preference. Love to a foster child is unconditional. I would have embraced being placed in a family who wanted me permanently, who anticipated my arrival and was excited to experience my first steps, my growth spurts, my voice changing, my first touchdown, and, hell, even my first girlfriend. I would have given anything to have experienced that.

The devastation you feel knowing someone didn't love you enough to want you or care for you is heart wrenching. I challenge you to ask about my ancestry when I've spent so much time lying helplessly in bed, praying someone would love me enough to take me home. I used to dream of the day that somebody, anybody, wanted little ole me. Many other foster kids, even the hard-core ones, prayed for the same thing often. All I wanted was someone who loved me and wanted to embrace me as their little boy.

You see, as an adult I wouldn't have changed any of Mama's punishments. I realize the love she had for me and that she expressed it in the best way she could. She ruled with a firm hand because she wanted the best for all of her children. Looking back on my childhood with Mama, I appreciate every beating, every punishment, and, most of all, the love she had for me to make sure I would become the man I am today. I am the man she intended me to be. And I am thankful.

If you didn't have what society says is a traditional family, with a mother and a father in the household, it's important to know that just because you didn't have that, it shouldn't make you feel less than anyone else. If the odds are stacked against you, dig in deep and define who you are. It is easier said than done, but if you are a fighter and have a chance, I encourage you to fight and change your negative experiences into positive ones.

Most importantly, you become the judge, jury, and decider of your own future. So many times people give up because of life's circumstances. I am here to tell you that you are important to yourself and to never underestimate what God's mercy can do for you and, most importantly, allow you to do in your future. I am the man I am today, and I am proud of who I am. If God gives you breath, you have to make the best out of the gift he has given you. If there is no one to encourage you, encourage yourself, but be proud of who you are, because God makes no mistakes.

You see, no matter your beginning, you have the authority as a young man or woman to determine your destination in life. I am still that little boy that no one wanted. I am the same little boy who didn't get a hug from his mother; I'm also the little boy who never had the chance to be introduced to his father, because he didn't even know I existed. But God saw fit to guide my steps. I'm the same little boy with the same DNA who decided he wanted to be somebody. I'm no better than any other foster child that was placed in the system. But as long as God gives you breath, you have a choice.

Neil Washington came a long way from the naysayers who thought I wouldn't amount to anything because I was a foster child. I came a long way from a young man who never got a chance to hug his mother other than on a cold slab, but most importantly, I came a long way from letting my own mother tell me I wasn't her son, that I was confused, and that she would rather move away than accept me. But God knew that one day her words would come back to bring us together, if only for a moment, and that I would have to help my sister lay her to rest with all the respect she deserved.

Yes, she was a woman not confused but determined not to get to know a son who would have given her the sky and the earth. Well, maybe I did; I pray once she left the earth, through her mistakes and misgivings, she went home to God. Who knew I would be the one to help bring that to pass? Well, call it the gift or call it fate, but somehow I knew I would be the man I am today. But I'm a man still standing by the grace of God, and if I may say so myself, I didn't turn out too damn bad.

All I can say is I thank God for giving me my life, my wife, and my children, but most of all, the gift of forgiveness. See, my advice to anyone is to never let someone steal your joy; it's not theirs to steal. Never let someone steal your favor, and never let bitterness control your heart. Your heart is sacred, and only you can determine what and how much control you will allow someone to have over it. I'm only a country boy, but I refused to let anyone steal what was given to me, and that was the gift that allowed me to enjoy my life. Yeah, maybe it didn't start off too great, but as long as see light of another day you are in control. My advice is to keep pushing, keep moving, but most of all, keep praying. God is always listening, and even his angels keep an ear out.

I encourage anyone, especially a foster child, since that was my circumstance but not who I was. I refused to let anyone other than God guide my path or stifle my desire for success. Sometimes you have to encourage yourself if there is no one else. You have to depend on the one who will never leave your side, and as you know, it is humanly impossible to leave yourself.

It all starts with determination to define your own destiny. Don't let your life's obstacles define you. Follow your dreams, but most of all, follow your heart. Greatness is a mirror image away. My advice not only to foster children but anyone who is dealing with life's challenges, stay true to God and, most importantly, seek his guidance and promise yourself that you will give this great gift of life that has been given to you all you got. Today is the beginning to achieve every gift with your name on it. "As long as I have breath in my body, I can make a bad day into a good day."

If I may say so myself, Neil Washington came a long way. Well, thanks for walking with me through my journey!

Hold on, Neil, the story does not end here. Let me introduce myself. I am Wayne; I am real, but only to God. You could see me when you needed protection from Ms. Thompson. During the beatings I took for you, I was your safety net. I left that note in the hospital, but it still didn't register. It wasn't supposed to.

How do I explain this? I shielded you from whatever God allowed me to. By all means, you did not walk this journey alone. Remember "Incoming, First Sergeant"? Oh, that was real too, but God decided to make sure you retired from the military so that you would not suffer the same fate as so many of your fallen comrades that you pray for daily.

When Ms. Thompson beat you, my gift would take you to that quiet place while I endured those for you. Oh, they were your beatings, and you could definitely see them, because they were actually happening to you. But God had bigger things for you to do, Neil, and he still does, so I endured the beatings and the pain of the favoritism you didn't receive that your foster brother got at times so that you would build up a hardened shell and wouldn't become a bitter young man.

In other words, God did not want you to become so traumatized by your ordeal that it would taint you for the rest of your life. Although your foster mother was wonderful in her own right, she taught you some important lessons that you carry with you until this day. Respect, hard work, and so many other wonderful values; you've said yourself that you loved her and were happy she was your mother, and to be honest, Neil, she was a wonderful lady. You wouldn't have turned out as wonderful as you are today had Ms. Thompson not started your foundation. Although it was hard, you were worthy. Sometimes we look upon a hard life as misfortune, but sometimes in God's eyes it's fortunate.

You have a story to tell, and only you can tell it. Believe it or not, you have already started telling your story and begun your journey with people you've met, soldiers you've led, and people you've just had conversations with, so continue, my brother, and know that your mission is much larger, as you will see. Do not let God down. No one grieved for me when I committed suicide but you, because I was not of this earth. Yes, the suicide was real, you felt the grief and the hurt, but that was another avenue God wanted you to explore so that you could feel that pain and never look at that as being a choice.

Remember the day when I ran from Officer Jones and Mr. Beal? That was going to be you. You witnessed all of that so it would strengthen you. There was no Officer Jones or Mr. Beal. Oh, they were real to you, but only you saw them because they were angels too. They were there to comfort you and let you know to hold on because there were individuals out in this world who would help you the way they did me. But I had to leave you traumatically so you could always remember that pain and never want to emulate my choice, and that devastation strengthened you.

Let's be clear: Do not question God, and know that what he does doesn't have to make sense. He's God! When he speaks, I listen, and you were the little boy I was sent to protect until I was told to move on to my next soul. I was taking this journey for you, but eventually I had to let you go and let you start becoming your own man. It was time to say good-bye; my job was done. So when you grieved for me, you were the only one grieving when you were young. I was your comforter. Sometimes Ms. Thompson, Eric, and the others wondered what you were thinking and who you were talking to. Little did they know you were going through the journey but at the same time being groomed to become the man you are today.

The neighbors, Ms. Thompson, Eric, and all the others had no time to grieve because they never saw me or were introduce to me. Listen and hear me loud and clear: do not question the power of what God can and will do; after all, he is the master. Again, what he does doesn't have to make sense to mere humans, but he always knows best, even in devastation when we ask God "Why, God?" Sometimes we will never know. And guess what? It's his decision to tell us or not.

We do not have to understand it; all we have to do is follow his lead. However, I was to show you all of those negative journeys that were so easy for you to take; you could have easily gone down either path—the suicide, the drug dealer, the hopeless young man—but we all have someone in our heart, head, and soul we just have to tap into and believe in.

What is one of your famous sayings? "Get thee behind me, Satan." And he flees, little brother, and you will always be my brother.

So in the beginning, that is why I asked, do you believe in God? If you do not, then you will never believe my story. But if you do, please walk with me through life and then death. God has given me the gift of journaling my life from the womb until now. Sorry, brother, it was not you journaling anything; it was your story told through me. I was your protector against the world until God felt you were fully capable. And Neil, my hat's off to you, because you have become a hell of a man, husband, father, and soldier. God told me I did my job well, and that's all I need to hear.

Come close, I have something to tell you. Your mother is looking down on you once again, thanking you as she did when you were that little boy sitting outside when you were in trouble and had those flashbacks and visions of your children, soldiers, and inspirational people that would eventually come into your life. Remember, the older lady thanking you for everything you had done was your mother, and you realized it at the funeral parlor. Well, she is still thanking you, Neil. She may not be here on earth to hug you, but every once in a while when you feel an extra tug, it's your mother letting you know she is forever grateful and proud of you!

Wishing she had given you a chance when you contacted her in that letter twenty-seven years ago. But you stay the course and do right by God the way you've been doing, because he just told me you shall see her beautiful face again and her arms will open happily. And you will hear the words you longed to hear for so long: "I love you, SON!" You will hear; trust me, I have never let you down—or should I say God has never let you down. Again this may not make sense now, but one day when you talk to God personally, it will.

Well, my job is truly done. It was nice being your brother and your guardian angel and, most of all, loving you. Let me ask you one thing before I go. Tell me, Neil, what do *you think you will say when you reach those loved ones who have passed on? Never mind, save it for that special day. I will hear it, you can believe that. I have ridden out the worst, and you can best believe I will be there when the greatest is handed out. What is it you used to say in the military? I loved it...HOOAH. Continue to stay strong and blessed, my brother. It was an honor serving you!*

Made in the USA
Middletown, DE
17 November 2014